KILLER GENES

Published in Great Britain by
Inside Pocket Publishing Limited
First published in Great Britain in 2011

A CIP catalogue record for this book is available from
the British Library

ISBN 978-0-9562315-7-4

10 9 8 7 6 5 4 3 2

Inside Pocket Publishing Limited Reg. No. 06580097
Printed and bound in Great Britain by
CPI Bookmarque Ltd, Croydon

www.insidepocket.co.uk

KILLER GENES

by C T Furlong

an arctic⁶
adventure

INSIDE POCKET

Also by C T Furlong
Killer Strangelets

To my parents – thank you for the genes.

Prologue

G20 Summit – London, July 12th

The choirmaster raises his baton. The boys and girls of the Suffolk East Children's choir begin their repertoire of old favourites. The delegates nod in time, their smiles just a bit stiff. The singing isn't the best in the world, but these men and women believe in encouraging young people.

In the front row, one man – olive skinned with shiny dark curls – coughs lightly then searches his pockets. Smiling apologetically, he pulls out his handkerchief, just in time to muffle a next, louder cough. His shoulders move up and down and tears roll down his face. Finally, admitting defeat, he rises from his seat, apologising as he makes his way to the exit.

Safely outside the doors, he succumbs to the overwhelming urge to void his lungs. His loud barking can be heard even above the crescendo of the song's finale.

The delegate in the next seat looks worriedly towards the door. Should he disturb the performance to check if the man needs help? As he stands up, a strange sensation develops in his stomach. He has to fight the wave of nausea, flowing like a ribbon from the middle of his torso to his throat. Realising he can't, he bolts for the door, shocking some of the audience as he staggers past. Heads turn, and murmurs of concern ripple through the crowd.

The small choir pauses as the audience applauds. When they begin the next song, sounds of squeaking can be heard. Several delegates in the front row squirm in their seats. The only lady in that row leans back heavily, her head rolling to the side.

Her nearest neighbour looks at her, concerned. Her face has drained of colour and beads of sweat bubble up on her forehead. He turns to look behind him. Almost everyone in the room is either clutching their stomach or fighting to control coughing fits. Something is wrong.

Without hesitation, he takes control. Raising his hand to silence the children, he turns to his aide.

'Get a medical team in here now!'

'Yes, Mr President!' The aide jumps to attention, speaking into his security microphone.

The President rises to his feet. Who needs his help the most? The lady beside him? The man gasping for breath beside her?

Behind him, another man slumps forward, clutching his chest. Is he having a heart attack? As he leans over to help the man, the President feels a stabbing pain in his left temple. The sharp pain shoots through his head, like a needle piercing to the very centre of his brain.

The sound of footsteps in the hallway grows fainter as his rising pulse booms in his ears. His vision blurring, he tries to focus on the person moving towards him. The uniform looks green. The man leans closer in. The emblem comes into focus – a red cross!

'No! Get back!' shouts the President.

'Sir!' the medic protests.

'Seal... off... the... area,' pants the President, feeling his knees hit the floor.

Around him, the British Prime Minister, the Russian President, and all the other G20 leaders are already unconscious on the floor.

'Call MI6... need to quarantine...' gasps the President, struggling to remain conscious. 'And... get a doctor in... here... now!'

1

Arctic6blog 1

After our last adventure, I've decided that no matter where I go now, I go *prepared*!

Consequently, in my bag are – well you can probably guess most of it: one of those fancy camping multi-tools, an all-singing all-dancing first-aid kit and plenty of emergency chocolate rations, but there are a few extra items, the most import being my iPad. I've also got my teeny tiny sWaP NOVA smartphone. It's about the size of a key ring, so that'll go in my pocket.

After all, it *was* technology that helped us to stop a mad woman from blowing up the planet last year. We wouldn't have even got inside CERN (European Centre for Nuclear Research – in English!) without it.

Iago's given me an important mission this time. I'm the 'official' blogger for this adventure. When I say adventure – I actually mean holiday. I'm pretty much willing to bet that nothing's going to happen on this holiday. You know why? 'Cause we're in Suffolk. Hardly the centre of the universe... I don't think anything ever happens here. Oh wait – there goes a horse. See what I mean? I live in hope, though. My stomach gets all fluttery at the slightest whiff of excitement.

Anyway, from today on, I, Tara Johnson, promise that you will have up-to-date and on-time blogs, no matter where we go or what we do. If *anything* should happen this time, you'll be right there – in the thick of it with me.

Oh wait a minute, I've just read back what I've written. I've started this all wrong. You probably don't know anything about the mad woman who tried to blow up the world, using the Large Hadron Collider at CERN. Or how, together as The ARCTIC6, me, my older brothers Cam and Renny, my cousins Iago and Aretha, and our friend Charlie stopped her. Well, we did have a little help from some of Renny's geek friends around the world, including the infamous hackers – the Greek Security Team.

By the way – just because I'm a girl and I'm blogging, don't for one minute think it'll be girly. I don't do chicklit, so I definitely won't do chickblog. I'd do anything most boys would. I'd jump out of a plane, white water raft, climb up the side of a building. Well... I say I would! I haven't actually *done* all or *any* of the above – but I would. Nothing would stop me! Er – apart from my size – maybe. Let's just say I'm on the small side of tiny.

Cam, Renny, and I arrived last night. I still can't quite believe that Mum and Dad let us come here alone. This is the first time they have trusted us to take care of ourselves. They're going hillwalking in the Lake District with my aunt and uncle. They said that the mobile phone signal's not great around there, but they'll check in when they can. I can't imagine that we'll need to contact them though.

My cousins, Iago and Aretha, will be here at lunchtime and we're going to have three whole days before the parents get here. It's such a shame that Charlie isn't coming. It'd be so great to have the ARCTIC6 back together again.

Anyway, I've got to go and get some food. I don't know what the plans are, but Iago asked us all to bring our bikes, tents, and sleeping bags. So I *know* we won't be sleeping in this holiday chalet for the next few days. Can't wait to find out what he's got planned.

Don't go anywhere. Or at least don't go too far. Now that I've got an iPad, I could take you to the shops with me but somehow, I don't think you'd find it that interesting.

Don't worry though, wherever we go after today, I'll take you. You won't miss a thing. Well maybe you will miss the actual cycling and the countryside. But the important stuff – I promise to deliver!

Arctic6blog 2

Renny here!

Listen, it's cute that Tara's taking her job as roving reporter so seriously but well, there has to be someone who can deliver in-depth scientific analysis and explain serious technological information, when the time comes. And we all know who that will be – don't we?

Well, for those of you who don't know, I am – how shall I put it? I'm the science whizz. I'm the brains of the operation. Sure, the others play their part, but I'm the one making the play, moving the pieces on the board, staying one step ahead of the game!

By the way, I'm tracking a strange webcast. You should check it out. There's something hinky going on in Somalia. I've just been watching the reporter Evan Andrews live, and everywhere he goes he finds people struck down by some weird virus. For now, it's only isolated pockets, but the mortality rate looks scary – like one hundred per cent. Anyway, I'll keep a close eye on it and get back to you with updates.

Can't wait for Iago to get here though. He said we were going to investigate a legend surrounding an Anglo-Saxon hoard. He wouldn't give me any further info. I've done a quick search on anything of interest round here and, apart from some old coins being dug up in a place called Dallinghoo recently, I can't find anything. I'm intrigued though.

Renny – intrepid science reporter – signing off.

✕🔒●●⊖

Arctic6blog 3

Unbelievable! I go out for a half an hour and it's open blogging season. My brother is the pits. You know, I'm given a job, which I take very seriously, and as soon as I turn my back every Tom, Dick and *Renny* thinks he can have a go!

I'm going to have a serious chat with Iago about Renny when he gets here!

Arctic6blog 4

I spoke to Iago and we came to an agreement: I will remain the 'official' blogger although if necessary, Renny can explain some of the technobabble.

Anyway, I'm so excited! We leave this afternoon. Renny was on the right track – we're going to Dallinghoo. Not long ago someone found half a million pounds worth of treasure in a field there. I know that lightning never strikes twice but well – you never know what we might find.

Arctic6blog 5

Hey there. Tara's back. Just to let you know where we are, and what we're up to...

Against the odds, we got our bikes onto the train on time – just. Of course, Renny was late, as usual. After we had all managed to drag our bikes up the steps and onto the platform, he decided he needed to go back to the shop for something. Who knows what he could have needed so badly? But that's just typical Renny.

After we'd loaded our bikes, Cam spent a lot of time begging the train guard to hold on as long as he could. The situation was getting desperate and I was seriously thinking of pinching Aretha. I know that sounds mean, but I was hoping that her hysterical crying might have some effect on the guard. Lucky for Aretha, an extremely red-faced, panting-and-puffing Renny raced up the steps to the platform, his bike slung over his shoulder like a bag.

'RENNY!' Cam shouted so loudly that Aretha jumped beside me, making me jump in sympathy like a Mexican wave.

I looked at Aretha and we leapt aboard the train, as fast as our legs could carry us. No way did we want to be shouted at like that. Huffing and sweating, Renny made it to the open door of the train's bike-storage carriage.

'Get in!' shouted the guard and we saw Renny's head disappear behind the sliding door. Poor Renny, he definitely wasn't getting bumped up to first class on *this* train.

Looking across the table at Iago, I could see that he was chuckling quietly. That was all it took to set me off. It started as a slow snigger, but built up inside me until I couldn't hold it in any more. I burst out laughing, followed a split second later by Iago. Then Aretha and Cam joined in. We laughed so hard that Aretha almost choked on the mint she was sucking, and Iago had to wipe the tears from the corners of his eyes.

When his phone rang, he was still chuckling, but his face changed instantly as he listened to whoever was on the other end.

'When?' was all he said.

He listened for another couple of seconds, then mumbled, 'OK,' and hung up. We all waited with bated breath. Not one of us dared to speak. He hung his head. Curiosity was eating me. I could feel it like a knot in my stomach.

'Well?' I asked.

'Charlie's coming...' he mumbled.

I didn't know what to say. This was better news than I could have hoped for. I could feel the grin spread across my face. When I looked at Aretha, she was smiling too.

'Yes!' I cheered. 'The ARCTIC6 all together again!'

Now that we were going to be reunited, I just knew that *something* was going to happen!

2

'Well, where are we going to meet her?' I asked.
'She'll call when her train arrives at Ipswich,' Iago replied.

I smiled at Aretha and she beamed back at me. Charlie was like a big sister to us, and I felt happy that she was coming along.

Iago sat quietly staring out the window most of the way, and Cam was reading, so I chatted with my younger cousin. Before long, the train arrived at Campsea Ash station.

I can't describe to you how 'in the middle of nowhere' that train station is. It *is* actually halfway between two villages. Maybe they thought that putting the train station in one of them would offend the people in the other. But, I still can't see why you'd put a train station in a place where everyone has to travel at least three miles to get to it.

With the help of the guard, we got all our bikes off the train. A very dusty, sweaty Renny was finally ejected from his 'cabin'. Aretha grinned and strolled off with her bike. Slinging my rucksack on my back, I followed her.

The warm sun bathed the tops of our heads and

shoulders as we left the station. Dappled light flickered through the trees on either side of the small country road and the warm-scented soil crunched under our feet. A cheeky little bird hopped from branch to branch above us. He jumped up and down madly. His loud whistle was probably his way of warning us to stay away from him.

Shading my eyes from the sun, I smiled up at him. 'Don't worry, little guy, we're just passing through. Your nest is safe, I promise.'

With that, he whistled even louder, making Aretha and I giggle.

'That's a great tit,' came Renny's voice from behind us. 'They're very territorial. Chase off anything that comes near them, no matter how big.'

'Tell me about it,' Aretha laughed. 'Thought he was going to dive-bomb us for a minute.'

'Yeah, he was thinking about it,' chuckled Renny. 'What a great start, eh? Should be lots to see today.'

Boy, did he have *no* idea how right he was!

Hopping on his bike, Renny started off happily down the inviting country road. Aretha and I mounted our bikes but decided to wait for Cam and Iago. Although we all love Renny, he isn't exactly the person you'd want to follow into the unknown. We were only a couple of seconds behind him though, so we wouldn't lose him.

Cam tapped the GPS coordinates into his phone and slotted it into its bike attachment. Slowly, we all set off after Renny.

The sky was powder blue and the sun splashing through the shady trees tickled my skin. I lifted my arms from the handlebars and soaked up the loveliness, as

I raised my face to the sun. This was the *most* perfect day – ever!

'Turn right,' Iago shouted to Renny, who had stopped at a junction.

My daydream melted away.

'Why are we turning here?' I asked.

Looking back over his shoulder, he shouted, 'Because we're going to Dallinghoo. Remember?'

'Oh!' I said, surprised. 'Are we there already?'

'Just about,' replied Iago, pointing at the crossroad's sign.

'Funny,' said Cam, slowing down, 'the sign says one mile, but according to the GPS we're still one and a half miles from Dallinghoo!'

Iago smiled. 'Now that you mention it, Dad warned me about Suffolk miles. He said that you can walk a mile in Suffolk and still be a mile away from where you want to be. Lucky we've got GPS then, eh?'

'Race you there,' cried Renny, tearing off before anyone could react.

With no more than a glance at each other, Cam and Iago both sprang into action.

'Boys!' smiled Aretha, digging in her bag. 'Want an apple?'

'Yeah – why not?' I said, taking one and pushing off slowly. 'They'll have to wait for us!'

We both munched our apples, pedalling lazily along the country road. Pity we couldn't carry on at this pace – it was so relaxing.

I finished my apple and chucked the core onto the green verge, to biodegrade naturally.

'Suppose we'd better find them,' I said, pedalling

harder.

'Yeah,' sighed Aretha. 'Shame – I like going at this pace.'

'Me too,' I replied.

We had only gone about a half a mile when we saw the boys up ahead. Renny was sitting by the roadside, with Cam and Iago standing over him.

From the look of Renny, I could guess what had happened. Dried grass poked out of his hair and his knees were gashed and bleeding.

'Did you bring a first-aid kit, Tar'?' asked Cam.

'I certainly did,' I replied proudly.

'Brilliant,' smiled Iago. 'Will you take a look at him?'

'Of course,' I said, taking a bottle of water from my bag.

After a bit of a clean, I could see that the wounds were not too big and none was very deep. Spraying disinfectant on them, I cut the roll of plaster to the right size to cover the bigger ones.

'Thanks sis',' smiled Renny, who hadn't made a sound during the treatment.

'Brave boy,' I said, ruffling his hair.

Walking over to Cam and Iago, I grinned. 'Well our wounded soldier's good to go!'

'Bike's not,' mumbled Cam.

'Don't suppose you've got a hammer in there?' asked Iago, pointing to my bag.

'Oh no – failed at the second hurdle. Why didn't I think of bringing a hammer?' I hit myself in the forehead, slapstick style and everyone laughed.

I'd thought I'd packed so well. Who'd have thought that Renny's bike would end up so bent we'd need a hammer?

'Oh well, we'll have to walk the last mile or so,' sighed Cam.

'What about asking at that little cottage?' Aretha said.

She was pointing to a small pale pink cottage, set into the woods, a little further up the road.

Leaving our bikes by the gate, we all started up the overgrown path. We could just make out the small house through the untended rose bushes and huge horse-chestnut trees.

A large, scruffy, growling dog stopped us before we got near to the door. He might have once been white, but his hair was so matted and dirty that he looked grey. His unusual blue eyes flitted about nervously from one to the other of us. He began pacing up and down in front of us and baring his teeth. He was doing his best impression of a guard dog, but you could tell that his heart wasn't in it. Iago pulled out a biscuit from his bag and threw it down. The dog stopped pretending straight away and ran to the biscuit.

Smiling at the rest of us, Iago winked, 'Old dogs – old tricks!'

He approached the front door. The paint was peeling and when he knocked, flakes of it fell off and drifted to the ground by his feet.

The loud rattle of a very large key in a very old lock made him step back a pace. Slowly the door creaked open onto a shadowy, cobwebbed hallway. Like a pressure lock on a submarine, it seemed to draw air in, before blowing it out again, along with years of dust. We all strained to see into the darkness. As we did, the outline of a figure came into view. A very old lady stepped out into the light.

'Um... hello,' asked Iago. 'Do you have a hammer we could borrow?'

'Come, come,' she almost whispered, beckoning us forward.

She seemed harmless enough, so we all moved closer.

'Let me see your eyes,' she said softly.

She was starting to creep me out, with her hypnotic voice. I felt like a sailor being lured to my death by a mermaid's song. But I carried on walking towards her anyway. Long grey hair hung around her shoulders and deep wrinkles surrounded her eyes.

She reached her hand out. Taking hold of my chin, she tilted my face towards her.

'Brown,' she muttered, moving on to Iago.

'Brown,' she muttered again before drawing Cam in.

'Brown – good,' she nodded this time.

She just smiled at Aretha before settling on Renny.

'Hazel – still good,' she said finally.

'Good, good, good,' she mumbled to herself, turning back towards her door.

'What's good?' asked Iago, frowning.

'The eyes,' she replied, looking back over her bony shoulder. 'None of you has blue eyes. You'll be safe if you're staying around here, tonight.'

Renny was turning his finger in circles next to his head. She definitely seemed a bit bonkers. Suddenly, I remembered why we were there.

'The hammer,' I hissed at Iago.

'Oh yeah! Um, excuse me. About the hammer — do you have one? You see we need to fix Renny's bike...'

She had already turned away and started closing the

door. Like a delay on a satellite news feed, she seemed to hear his words a couple of seconds late. She stopped and thought before answering, 'Try the shed at the back.'

And without another word, she shut the door in our faces.

3

'How weird,' said Aretha, looking around, 'I feel like I was just under a spell – do you?'

'Yeah, her voice was kind of hypnotic,' replied Cam.

'She gave me the heebie jeebies,' I said, scrunching up my shoulders, trying to shake off the feeling.

'Hmm,' mumbled Iago, walking around the side of the little cottage.

Renny, following close behind, just raised an eyebrow and smirked. Nothing fazes Renny, no matter how weird. He just grins through most things. He has his own 'secret smile' inside him; must be a nice thing to have.

'Shall we all come?' I asked.

'The more the merrier,' said Cam, sauntering after them.

Tugging my arm, Aretha whispered, 'I don't really want to go round there.'

She looked frightened. That old lady had really spooked her. When I thought about it, I didn't actually want to go either. Even though it was really warm, I was suddenly chilly. I felt as if something cold had slipped into our perfect day.

'Probably nothing but weeds and broken stuff there

anyway,' I replied, pulling her back towards the garden gate.

The dog scampered out from behind a bush, stopping us in our tracks. Although he wasn't growling or snarling, we still felt threatened. His eyes never left us as he paced back and forth across the path. Then he stretched out his legs and slowly lay down just in front of us. Aretha stepped slightly behind me. I didn't mind; I was the older one and should be braver.

The sneeze that erupted from the dog shook him and me. I squealed. It was only a little one, but it was still a squeal.

'Bless you,' came Aretha's voice from behind my left ear. Laying his head on the ground, he whimpered softly. The dog seemed to be feeling sorry for himself.

'Ahh – poor thing. Maybe he's feeling ill,' said Aretha.

'Aretha, you were terrified of him ten seconds ago. Now you're worried about his health?'

'Well, I didn't know he was sick then, did I?'

'Anyway, we haven't got any doggy medicine, so there's nothing we can do for him,' I replied.

Stepping out from behind me, Aretha moved slowly towards the dog, and squatted down in front of him. Taking off her rucksack, she shuffled through it until she found what she was looking for.

'Voila!' she said smiling, as she put the biscuit down in front of the dog's nose. 'It's not medicine but I'm sure it'll make you feel better.'

The dog perked up straight away, downing the biscuit in one gulp.

'You old ham actor,' smiled Aretha, rubbing his head.

He let out a small growl of approval, then rolled onto his back. As Aretha was tickling his tummy, the three boys emerged from behind the house. Iago, hammer in hand, strolled past us towards the gate. Aretha stood up and we all trailed after him. Turning to close the gate behind us, I noticed the dog following.

'Back, boy,' I said pointing towards the house.

The dog hung his head and started skulking back and forth across the path, not making eye contact with me. As soon as I turned my back, he crept forward again. It was like a game of musical statues. Laughing, I closed the gate.

The boys already had the tyre off by the time we got to them. While Cam held the wheel steady, Iago beat it with the hammer. Soon it was straight enough so that it spun freely inside the frame.

Leaving the others to replace the tyre on his wheel, Renny ran back up the garden path to return the hammer. I looked around, curious; the dog was nowhere to be seen. *Probably gone back inside*, I thought, and as Renny returned, we all jumped on our bikes and set off on the last leg of our journey.

I don't know why, but I had the strange sensation of being followed. I turned my head a couple of times to check and I thought I saw some movement. Was it just a bird?

'Come on, Tara,' shouted Iago.

I was lagging behind. No matter how curious I was, I didn't want to lose sight of the others.

The sun was starting to slip lower as we headed for a small stream Iago had marked on his map. I could hear him whistling. He sounded happy. I smiled. Who wouldn't feel happy on such a beautiful day?

4

Arctic6blog 6

We arrived at Iago's coordinates a half an hour ago, Thought I'd better update you.

This looks like a perfect spot to camp in. It's a clearing in a small wood, and there's a stream just beyond the trees. Charlie phoned from Ipswich. She's going to take a train to Woodbridge, which takes about fifteen minutes, and then get a taxi to here. We're only about five miles from Woodbridge, so that shouldn't take long either. She hasn't got her bike with her but she's going to borrow one from her aunt tomorrow. Charlie's Uncle Jim works for the air-sea rescue service and is based somewhere near here. Better blog-off for now and help get the tents up. Get back to you...

Arctic6blog 7

Renny here, guys.

Listen; just from a scientist's viewpoint, that weird old lady was talking gobbledegook. There is no reason on earth why eye colour should be linked to security in a countryside environment. That kind of mumbo-jumbo frightens people and actually, she should be ashamed of herself. I'm not going to sleep any more soundly tonight just because I've got hazel eyes. In fact, I'm hoping to do a bit of investigating once the sun goes down. I'm not expecting to find a hoard of Anglo-Saxon treasure, but there are lots of myths and legends about burials here. I'll let you know what I find.

By the way – that story that I've been following in Somalia – it seems that the virus is spreading faster than expected. I just checked Evan Andrews' webcast again and he's finding dead and dying people wherever he goes. He has even lost some of his local crew to it. So far *he* seems to be OK, but you can imagine he's pretty worried. I'll keep you posted.

Renny out...×■●●⊖

Arctic6blog 8

I agree with Renny. I don't think that grown-ups should say those kinds of things. They should know when to keep stuff to themselves.

I don't know if it's just me but I still have a creepy feeling that whatever I do, I'm being watched. Like just now, when I went down to the stream to wash out the pan for the baked beans, I heard a rustle in the bushes behind me. Probably just my imagination but still – if that old woman hadn't put the thought of danger in my head, I wouldn't be feeling like this.

Anyway, down to the important news: Charlie's here! Her taxi arrived about five minutes ago. You should have seen the look on the taxi driver's face. As I ran towards the road, I could hear him saying, 'You sure you want to get out *here,* love?'

Charlie looked at her phone and smiled. 'These *are* the coordinates.'

Stepping from the taxi, she dragged her rucksack, complete with rolled-up sleeping bag and ground mat, out of the back. From of the edge of the small wood, Aretha and I rushed her. Charlie shrieked happily, her blue eyes sparkling.

Dressed in khaki shorts and white vest she was so naturally lovely. In Charlie's case, it's true that what's on the inside shows on the outside.

Iago, who'd been busy with the fire, looked up as we neared the campsite. On seeing her, he smiled so broadly it almost looked forced. Charlie's shiny brown hair bounced around her tanned shoulders and even after the long train journey, she looked fresh and relaxed. She ran her hand gently over Aretha's hair as she listened to her recap of the day's events.

'Guess someone's going to have to protect me then,' Charlie said, when Aretha told her of the old woman's warning.

Iago cleared his throat and stood up. 'Just some old circus reject. Probably makes her money reading tea leaves.'

He busied himself with the fire and said no more.

'Hey Charlie! Just in time,' called Cam, stepping out from behind a small copse, arms laden with wood for the fire.

Charlie ran to help him and he seemed happy to see his oldest friend again.

'Really glad you could make it, Charl',' he said.

'Wouldn't have been the same without you.'

He put some wood on the fire before heading off to collect more for later.

Calling Aretha to help me, I set about opening the sausages and beans. Charlie sauntered up to where Iago was squatting by the fire.

'So, how *are* you, Iago?'

Iago cleared his throat, looking at her.

'I'm fine,' he replied.

Standing up and stretching, he yawned casually before turning away from her to search through his bag for something.

'Charlie!' shouted Renny, running across the campsite.

Like a puppy dog, he jumped on Charlie, hugging her affectionately. You can always count on Renny for an over-the-top response to any situation. When he finally let go of her, Charlie stepped back.

Renny launched straight into conversation. 'Did you hear about the blue-eyed thing, Charl'? It's really interesting. I was just thinking about it while I was collecting firewood and I think I might know why the old lady was so worried—'

'Renny,' smiled Charlie. 'I'm starving. Although I'd really love to hear about your theory, can it wait until after dinner?'

'Oh – but it might be important, Charlie,' he said. 'To you, anyway.'

'What might be?' she asked.

'Well... your blue eyes reminded me of the headline that I saw on the local newspaper. There's just been another disappearance in this area. Well – it might be just a runaway, but still...'

'What's that got to do with me?' asked Charlie.

'The headline was "Please Come Back My Blue-Eyed Boy",' he answered.

'Have there been others?' she asked. 'Did they have blue eyes too?'

'I don't know, but after what the old woman said...'

'Renny – you're frightening me,' said Charlie, a small smile on her lips.

'Oh, don't be frightened Charl'. I'm sorry. It's probably nothing. Let's just forget I mentioned it. OK?'

'OK,' she said, and Renny headed back to his laptop.

Charlie, Aretha, and I busied ourselves with cooking the sausages and beans while the boys dug around in the fire for the potatoes they'd buried as soon as they'd lit the fire. On our last camping trip, Dad had wrapped potatoes in tinfoil and buried them in the hottest part of the fire. It made them nice and smoky on the outside but soft and delicious on the inside.

'C'mon, let's eat,' I called as soon as the sausages were ready.

Within seconds, everyone was sitting around the fire, plates on laps. Iago handed out the potatoes while Aretha circled around us, dishing out spoonfuls of slightly smoky baked beans. Sharing the sausages equally, I left two in the pan, for seconds. I grinned at Renny as my brother wolfed his food down. I had a very good idea who might be having *those* seconds.

We ate in total silence. For some reason, a meal cooked on a campfire is so much tastier than home-cooked food. The smell of wood smoke and warm food in your belly as you look forward to a night's camping is probably one of the best feelings I know. It should be on your list of twenty things to do before you die.

Washing up after cooking on a campfire is not high on anyone's list, so we drew straws. Renny and Charlie drew the short ones, so they set off towards the edge of the small stream. I could already hear Renny chattering away, always just one step behind Charlie, as if his talking interfered with his walking.

Cam helped Aretha and I to organise our tent. It was in the middle with the other two tents on either side. Suddenly a thought struck me – we had only three tents! Where would Charlie sleep?

'What's wrong, Tar'?' asked Iago.

'Uh... just wondering where Charlie is going to sleep is all,' I replied.

Without answering, Iago set about putting up his tent and organising his gear.

5

I heard Charlie's laugh before I saw her and Renny emerge from the wood. She had hardly set foot in the clearing when Iago headed towards her. Stopping short, she gazed up at him as he took one final step.

'You can have my tent,' he said looking down into her face.

'Where will you sleep, then?' she asked.

'Out here,' he replied.

'But what if it rains or gets cold?'

'No rain forecast for tonight,' Renny butted in.

'Thanks,' said Charlie. 'Hope you'll be OK out here.'

She lowered her head and a strand of hair fell forward. Iago reached up and slowly tucked it back behind her ear.

'I'll be fine,' he said, smiling. 'I like the stars.'

We hadn't brought pyjamas with us, but Aretha and I had brought tracksuits to sleep in – nice fleecy warm ones. We decided to wash ourselves and get changed before we lost the light completely. We didn't brush our teeth since we had a treat planned – we could do that later with bottled water.

When we arrived back, slightly cleaner and snugly dressed, I saw that Charlie had pulled on her sweatshirt and exchanged her sandals for socks and hiking boots. The boys had also pulled on their sweaters and built up the fire for the night.

Aretha delved in her rucksack, while I filled a pan with milk, setting it on the fire.

'Marshmallows anyone?' she called, dragging out the enormous bag of slightly squashed pink and white delights.

The others busied themselves with finding sticks as I measured out the cocoa into our tin camping cups. We all settled down, sipping our cocoa, silently watching the pink or white blobs on the ends of our sticks transform into crispy black skins with runny, sticky, gooey middles. The next bit is the hard bit. You have to be patient. Anyone foolish enough to put the marshmallow straight into their mouth must pay the price. The blisters on your tongue or the roof of your mouth can take many weeks to heal – believe me! I *have* been that fool...

With the bag of marshmallows more than half-empty, Aretha yawned.

'I'm going to bed,' she said, and grabbed the bag. 'Don't think I'm leaving these here. They stay in my tent and anyone caught trying to steal them will be sorry!'

'Night, sis',' smiled Iago as Aretha bent over his shoulder and kissed him on the cheek.

'Night, bruv,' she replied, 'and don't stay up too late. You don't want to be too grumpy in the morning.'

Iago scowled at her. But we all know how grumpy he can be. He's definitely *not* a morning person. Charlie, who was right beside him, grinned and he turned away.

'Wait, Aretha,' shouted Renny, running off towards the trees.

After a few seconds he came running back, his arms filled with something.

'What's that?' asked Aretha, as he pushed some of it into her arms.

'It's heather.'

'What's it for?'

'It's for lying on. Here, let me show you.'

He headed off towards our tent. Lifting our roll mattresses, Renny spread the heather underneath.

'There you go,' he smiled, patting the mattresses back into place. 'You can't go camping and *not* sleep on heather. It just shouldn't be done!'

He seemed so passionate about it that Aretha just looked at me and smiled. When he'd finished, she climbed into her sleeping bag and turned on her camping light.

'It's... comfortable. Thanks,' she said. 'Now can I be left alone to read my book, please?'

'I won't be long,' I said, walking away. 'Just need to go clean the cups.'

'Oh, I'll help,' Renny said, catching me up.

'Thanks, Rens,' I replied.

I hadn't really wanted to go to the stream alone in the dark, but I felt silly asking someone to come with me. Cam, Charlie, and Iago shared a joke about something that had happened in science class as we walked away.

Renny was unusually silent as we rinsed the cups out in the cool, still water.

'What's up, Rens?' I asked him gently. 'You got something on your mind?'

'Yeah...' he said, turning towards me and frowning. 'I'm just a bit worried about Charlie, is all.'

'Why – because of that silly old woman?'

'It's just that I did some research. And it turns out that there have been two apparent runaways round here in the last week and both of them have blue eyes.'

'That might just be a coincidence, Renny,' I answered, as we began walking away from the stream.

'Might be, but after what she said...'

Just then, the bush in front of me rustled loudly. Startled, I flew to Renny's side.

'Shhhh,' whispered Renny, standing between me and whatever was lurking out there in the darkness.

He took one step backwards. Following his lead, I began to backtrack towards the stream. I had no idea what we would do when we got there, but it seemed like the best option at that moment. We could always wade across the stream and escape along the other bank.

The bushes rustled quietly again; this time whatever was in there was moving stealthily – stalking us! A wave of panic rose as the leaves at the front of the bush parted and a dark form began to emerge.

Renny yelped and turned on his heel. I was already in mid-flight and now I was one step ahead of him. Without a backward glance, I splashed straight into the freezing stream.

Renny's splashing behind me spurred me on. I didn't have time to worry about what I felt. I lifted my knees to quicken my pace. Round slimy stones met my feet as I plunged deeper into the stream. I felt my right foot slipping and had to force my left one forward, to steady myself. It arrived too late and I hung momentarily, like the leaning tower of Pisa – the angle all wrong.

I crashed sidelong into the water. Amazingly, given

that the stream was no more than one foot deep at the most, I managed to wet not only my entire body, but almost all my hair as well.

Spitting out water and grappling all round me for something to push off, I was shocked to see Renny passing me. Was he really going to leave me here at the mercy of some unknown predator? Scenes from films of velociraptors circling downed prey flashed before my eyes and I screamed, 'RENNY!'

Before Renny had a chance to come back and drag me heroically from the jaws of the terrible beast – there it was, by the water's edge, slowly lapping at the clear water. It lifted its head to stare at me.

'It's a *dog*, Renny – it's just a silly dog.'

Falling back in the water, I laughed until my hot tears mingled with the cold water on my face. Gasping for air as the waves of laughter subsided, I shivered and struggled to my feet. The dog growled a warning to me but I wasn't afraid of him now; he was nothing compared to the 'beast' of my imagination.

He turned his head away from me, but I'd seen that face before – he was the dog from the old lady's house. He *had* been following us! *He* was the cause of my terror, not to mention pain, cold and possible pneumonia – and here he was, acting as if he was just out for a night-time stroll in the woods. The look of 'Oh fancy meeting you here!' on his face made my blood boil.

'Bad dog,' I said angrily, approaching him. 'What are you doing here?'

To his credit, he stood his ground.

'Tar','said Renny, wading back out of the stream. 'I'm sure he'd like to tell you, but I think we've got more important things to deal with right now.'

He looked almost as wet as I did, considering he hadn't actually fallen into the stream. Renny could do that – when we were little, Renny would come home from school covered in mud even if rain had forced us to play indoors.

Looking down at myself miserably I answered, 'You're right,' and stepped away from the stream.

I hadn't taken three steps when the dog began a low gurgling growl. He looked past me and bared his fangs.

'What's he growling at now?' I asked.

Renny looked behind him, in the direction of the dog's gaze.

'Probably just a fox or a rabbit or something,' he said, shrugging his shoulders.

By now, my teeth were chattering. I was too cold to care. Looking down at the dog, I muttered, 'You coming with us then, Trouble?'

He seemed to take no notice of me. I shrugged.

'Suit yourself!'

The dog growled again, then gave a short quiet yelp. I turned, ready to moan at him to stop. Instead, my eyes were drawn to Renny, who was stepping into the cold stream again.

'What is it, Rens?' I asked.

'I don't know,' he whispered. 'I thought I saw something.'

'Like an animal or something?'

'No — like a weird light!'

6

'How can a light be weird, Renny?' I demanded, now shivering and desperate to get back to camp.

'I don't know,' he shrugged. 'It just glowed strangely – that's all. And the dog doesn't seem to like it either.'

'Listen, I vote we should go back and get changed. I'm frrreeeezing!'

I rubbed my arms to try to stop the shivering and picked up the cups.

'S'pose so,' mumbled Renny.

I could see his bottom lip quivering. I knew he felt every bit as cold as I did, no matter how curious he was. But Renny has an amazing ability to ignore discomfort if something grabs his attention.

'C'mon,' I said and grabbed his hand.

Making our way back through the undergrowth was hard. It seemed to take longer than I remembered. The added weight of water in our trainers and the fact that the sun had almost set slowed us down. Doing anything when you are cold and wet is harder.

'What on earth..?' said Cam, as Renny and I got closer to the light from the campfire.

Charlie jumped up to help us. We must have looked pathetic – like two bedraggled puppy dogs who'd followed a ball too far into the water. My bottom lip trembled with self-pity and I had to turn my face away, so the others couldn't see it.

'What happened to you?' asked Iago.

I tried to explain but my teeth were chattering so loudly, I couldn't.

'Let's get you out of these things,' said Charlie, leading me off.

Renny just stood there by the fire, dripping.

'Come on...' I heard Cam saying to Renny.

I couldn't get into the tent dripping wet, so I went around the side, while Charlie fetched my bag.

'What have you got to change into?' asked Charlie as I peeled off my dripping tracksuit.

'J... j... jeans...' I answered, the light breeze feeling very chilly to my soaked skin.

Aretha poked her head through the zip of the tent.

'What's going on?' she yawned.

'Tara and Renny had a small *incident*!' Charlie answered for me as I struggled into my jeans.

Aretha backed up into the tent and re-emerged a couple of seconds later with thick woolly socks that were already warm and toasty.

'Oh yes!' I said, as I felt the warmth creep all the way up to my frozen knees. 'Did you just take these off?'

Aretha nodded. She really would give someone the shirt off her back. As I pulled my wool jumper over my clean T-shirt, I began to feel better.

Aretha, Charlie, and I headed back to the campfire. Iago had put some water on the fire to boil and Cam was getting the cups organised.

'Good idea, Iago,' smiled Charlie. 'I think we could

all do with a warm cuppa!'

'Some more than others,' mumbled Renny, looking sorry for himself.

I could see that he was dressed completely in other peoples' clothes.

'Oh no, Renny – don't tell me that you didn't bring a change of clothes?' I asked.

Renny's grin said it all. Brilliant though he is – he's *not* good at looking after himself.

A very small, shy '*Woof*' came from the edge of the trees. In our self-pity and our need for comfort, Renny and I had almost forgotten the reason we had ended up in the stream in the first place.

'Awww,' said Aretha softly, approaching the dog gently. 'What are you doing here? Are you lost?'

The dog looked up into her gentle eyes and whimpered sadly; he's *such* an actor! She sat down, and he sidled up to her, nuzzling her hand.

'Oh! Oh!' stuttered Renny, bouncing up and down like a nervous meerkat.

'What?' asked Iago.

'We almost forgot to tell you about the weird lights.' Renny grinned, letting it hang.

'Come on, Renny,' said Iago rolling his eyes. 'Get to the point.'

'OK. OK... Well – after the dog, um... startled us, we saw a strange light coming from across the fields.'

'Quantify a *strange* light,' demanded Iago.

'Well,' Renny said. 'It was a strange colour – sort of blue-green.'

'Could be a polytunnel or something like that,' said Cam. 'You know one of those places where they force-grow tomatoes so we can eat salad all year round?'

'Yeah, but what's strange,' Renny continued, 'is that it was there one minute, then gone the next.'

'Hmmm,' said Cam. 'Maybe they turn on and off with some kind of timer?'

'Maybe,' mused Renny, 'but it looked kind of weird to me.'

Charlie, who'd been quietly tapping on her laptop as we sat there, suddenly laughed. Everyone stared at her. She nodded, holding her hand up.

'Wait... wait.'

'What is it, Charl'?' asked Iago.

'Well... while you were discussing it, I did a search for 'strange lights' and 'Suffolk' and just look at what I got.'

Swivelling her laptop round so that we could see it, she chuckled. It was a really crude drawing of an alien spaceship. It could have been drawn by a five-year old; it was saucer shaped and had little arrows pointing to various bits, describing the lights and other fixtures

'Doh!' muttered Renny, thumping his own forehead. 'Of course, the Rendlesham UFO incident... How could I have forgotten that? They call it the "British Roswell".'

'In fairness, Renny,' Charlie began, 'it *did* happen in 1980, so you weren't exactly around!'

'Yeah... I s'pose,' he said, sounding disappointed in himself.

Renny prides himself on knowing lots – especially all the *geek* stuff!

'Go *on* then. Tell us what you know,' sighed Cam.

We don't need encyclopaedias in our house. We only use Wikipedia if Renny isn't around. I suppose it has its advantages – you don't have to sift through twenty websites before you find what you're looking for!

'Well,' began Renny in a hushed voice, 'it happened in December 1980. An American security patrol, stationed at a barracks near Woodbridge, on the edge of Rendlesham Forest, reported seeing flashing lights near the east gate of the barracks. Some of the men even claim to have seen a hovering "ship" but of course, in true *X-Files* fashion, the men were silenced and the whole incident classified until 2001.'

'I don't think it was a UFO you saw,' Iago cut in.

Renny's shoulders slumped a little.

'But the dog was scared,' Renny replied.

Aretha continued petting the dog, as he sat there, cuddling up against her.

'I didn't say I didn't think it was worth investigating though,' smiled Iago.

Renny's eyes lit up. The merest whiff of an investigation gets Renny excited. The dream of another adventure had been on his mind since our last outing, at CERN. I'm afraid he might be disappointed this time – what could possibly be going on in sleepy Suffolk?

7

We finished our tea and biscuits as quickly as we could; we were all excited now. It didn't matter that none of us believed in UFOs, apart from Renny, of course. We were just happy to be out for a night-time skulk about. We readied our rucksacks, making sure we had torches, snacks, camping multi-tools, and mobile phones. Renny packed his smallest laptop and I made sure I had my iPad – the blogger's choice. Even Aretha had perked up and I could see the gleam in her eyes as she changed back into her day clothes.

The dog rambled around the campfire, waggling his tail idly. He glanced at me sideways once or twice as he did so. He was such a shady character. I had the feeling that this dog had learned to be sly. He pretended he wasn't interested, but he watched everything that was going on.

Suddenly, I felt a bit sorry for the poor thing; what kind of life had he led? Maybe he had learned that it was better for him to keep a low profile.

'Right!' Iago began. 'Everyone ready?'

We all nodded.

'OK, this may be just a night-time recce but we'll be out in the dark. It'll be tricky underfoot so please everyone – be careful. Rabbit burrows will probably be our biggest obstacle so please try *not* to fall down one. I don't want to have to carry anyone back to camp or, worse still, have to call for an ambulance. Tara – have you got the first-aid kit?'

I nodded and Iago carried on. 'We don't know what we're investigating so, if you haven't already done so; please switch your phones to vibrate. It'd be stupid to blow the whole operation because Mum decides to check up on us!'

Immediately Renny fumbled in his rucksack – of course he had forgotten to switch his phone to vibrate.

Iago turned to Cam.

'We'll use your phone for GPS,' he said, 'but please, everyone else – remember that this is a recce, so we only communicate when absolutely necessary. If this has something to do with UFOs and the military, we don't want them locating us before we discover what's out there. Though, if you ask me, this whole thing sounds like one of Charlie's favourite *X-Files* re-runs.'

Iago grinned widely, his teeth shining in the darkness.

'They can still track you, you know,' said Renny. 'Even when your phone is switched off. I've read that Big Brother has been forcing all mobile communications companies to install spy software in your phone that pings, whether your phone's on or off. They say it's just in case of emergencies.'

'What kind of emergencies?' I asked.

'Say, for example, there's a hurricane and the emergency services need to identify where they should search for trapped victims,' Renny answered. 'Well, the government just has to flick a switch to activate the software and they get a *ping* from every mobile phone in the area. I suppose it's quite clever since most people will have their mobile phone either on them or very nearby.'

'I can see where that would be quite helpful,' mused Charlie, 'but I can't imagine any government in the world being allowed to do such a thing. Surely it's an invasion of privacy?'

'Charlie, Charlie, Charlie...' laughed Renny. 'If you knew the things I've heard from my friends online. Invasions of privacy are *not* unusual. In fact, they happen every day.'

'Yeah... in hacker-land they do!' said Cam.

'Anyway,' Iago said. 'We're wasting time here. Tara, Renny – we'll follow you. Show us where you were when you saw the lights.'

Renny moved off and I trotted along behind him. Looking over my shoulder, I saw Iago placing his arm round Aretha, guiding her forward.

'Where's the dog?' he asked.

'I've left him by the campfire, nice and cosy,' she smiled. 'Do you think we should take him back to the old lady tomorrow?'

'I think so,' he replied.

Charlie caught up with them and linked arms with Aretha, smiling. Cam brought up the rear. In this formation, we entered the wood.

Trudging through the thick undergrowth was difficult now that night was upon us. The moon hadn't risen yet, so we had to pick our way slowly towards the stream. Brambles snagged at my trouser legs.

Renny stopped dead in front of me, holding up his

hand. Curiosity forced me forward. He shushed me as I came up behind his shoulder.

'What is it?' I whispered.

Holding his finger to his lips, he turned towards the others, waving them to be quiet.

Iago, leaving Charlie and Aretha behind, crept forward slowly, making no sound at all. When he reached us, Renny turned to him.

'What?' whispered Iago.

Renny held his finger up to shush Iago too. They didn't speak, but I could understand Renny's hand signals. He'd heard a noise dead ahead. Iago motioned to everyone else to crouch down where we were and hold our positions. Cam turned his back to us to check for anything approaching us from behind.

And we waited...

8

I couldn't be sure what I heard at first.

Looking around at the rest of the gang, I could tell that they had heard something too. I could feel the surge of adrenaline as it channelled its way around my veins. My body was ready for fight or flight.

To my right, Iago changed his position to a more attacking one – his back was now flat, his legs like a sprinter's in the starting blocks – ready to spring forward towards the threat.

Then we heard it. We *all* heard the same thing and froze.

The man's voice sounded like it was no more than ten feet in front of us. Renny had been right – there *had* been something out there. And when I heard what the man said, I knew that Renny had been right to be curious about the weird lights too.

'Nah — looks like just some kids camping. Camp's deserted now though... Yeah, I've set a few scares for them when they get back – should send 'em packing...'

There was cold venom in his voice. The chilly sensation I'd had earlier at the old lady's house came flooding back. I just had a feeling that there was something horrible out there somewhere.

I could hear the crackle of a two-way radio, as he turned away. Then the sound of shuffling undergrowth grew fainter as the creepy man headed back to wherever he'd come from. Iago relaxed a little and I breathed a sigh of relief. He gave each of us a swift glance then locked eyes with Charlie, smiling.

'He sounded like a security guard, or something,' I said.

'He did, but what kind of security guard sets up "scares" at campsites?' said Iago.

'Psssttt,' whispered Renny, holding up his phone. 'Take a look at this!'

'What is it, Renny?' whispered Iago.

Renny just handed him the phone. Cam joined us from his rear-guard position as Iago replayed the podcast. It was an audio-only podcast with a few stills thrown in for information. Renny passed around his Bluetooth earpiece and, one by one, we listened.

'After hours of enforced media silence, we're finally allowed to report on an extraordinary and devastating piece of news. At the G20 summit in London, some of the leaders of the world's twenty most powerful countries may have contracted a serious illness. They remain at the location and the building has been sealed off. Defra spokesperson, Tom White, has confirmed that his office has been contacted regarding a possible viral outbreak in Central London. At this moment, we are unable to confirm which of the leaders has been affected by the illness, but initial reports suggest that not everyone at the scene is showing symptoms. As soon as we have more news we'll update you.'

'Iago,' began Aretha timidly, 'do you think that was real?'

Iago turned towards his sister, his face serious.

'I think it was,' he said.

'What on earth is going on?' asked Charlie, thinking aloud. 'Of course, it might not be a virus. Could be just food poisoning. Probably some idiot didn't cook their sausages properly. Can you imagine being the chef responsible for poisoning the leaders of the twenty most powerful nations in the world? You might find it hard to get a job after a performance like that!'

'I don't know, Charlie,' began Renny, and then paused for an annoyingly long time.

'Renny?' hissed Cam.

'Oh!' said Renny, rejoining the real world. 'It's just that – it'd be really difficult to accidentally poison that many people. I mean, they'd have to have all eaten the same thing, which is a bit unlikely.'

His eyes glazed over and I knew his focus was gone again. Renny does that quite often; one minute he's there in the moment with you and the next, he's back inside his own head. I truly believe that my brother is a genius, but he can be a bit frustrating.

Then Renny came back to us, signalling us to move closer.

'Why would Defra be involved?' he whispered.

We all shrugged our shoulders. How would *we* know?

'You only call Defra when you need to quarantine somewhere. They wouldn't be called out unless there was compelling evidence.'

'What do you mean – "compelling evidence"?' asked

Charlie.

'Well they don't exactly investigate gone-off sausages, if you know what I mean.'

'So this wasn't food poisoning then!' Iago said.

'No – Tom White must be pretty sure that this *illness* is viral. Why else would he mention it? This can mean only one thing...'

'Biological warfare,' whispered Charlie.

9

We came to the edge of the small wood. We couldn't see the lights from here; there must have been something blocking our view, so we followed Renny's directions.

Trudging across the open heath-land, I listened to Charlie and Renny swapping ideas or questions about the attack. Charlie's almost as interested in science as Renny is, though she doesn't talk about it quite as much.

'Do you think this really was an attack?' I asked them.

'It's highly unlikely that *all* the world leaders would come down with a normal virus at exactly the same time,' answered Renny. 'This had to have been planned.'

'But *who* would do such a thing and *why*?' I asked.

'If you were a madman and you wanted to bring the world to its knees, the easiest way to do it would be to just take out its leaders and their finance ministers,' said Charlie.

While I was still at stage one, i.e. the *why*, Renny and Charlie were moving on to the *how*.

'What about delivery methods?' asked Charlie.

'Remember the sarin gas attack on the Japanese underground?' I heard Renny saying.

'Oh yeah,' answered Charlie. 'Do you think this could have been released in gas form?'

'No,' answered Renny, after a second's pause. 'Absolutely not!'

'Why not?' I asked.

'Yes – why not?' echoed Charlie.

'C'mon – think about it for a minute!'

I did, but I couldn't come up with an answer.

'Because everyone would have become ill...' answered Charlie.

'Ah,' I said, finally understanding. 'If the virus was released in a gas cloud, then everyone who was there at the time would have become sick!'

'But *not* everyone who was there is showing symptoms,' Charlie said.

'True,' said Renny.

The moonlight highlighted the frown on my brother's face, making him look older than his years. It was as if he carried the world on his shoulders.

'What is it, Rens?' I asked.

'It's just that, to be honest, I can't imagine *how* they delivered the virus.'

'Hey guys.'

Iago's voice behind me made me jump. We were all so in the moment that we hadn't even heard him approach.

'Iago!' groaned Charlie quietly. 'You scared the hell out of me!'

'What were you three up to anyway?' he asked.

'We were just wondering *how* the virus was delivered to the G20 members,' answered Renny.

'Yeah – weird, huh?' said Iago. 'Wish there was

something we could do to help!'

'We're not a lot of good to anyone, stuck out here in the middle of nowhere,' I added.

'They'll figure it out,' said Charlie, hopefully. 'I mean, they have the most highly qualified people on the planet, all working together to figure this out. They'll find a solution. And they'll get the best medical care in the world. I'm sure there are doctors being flown in from here, there, and everywhere, as we speak.'

'I don't know,' said Renny negatively. 'I've just got a bad feeling about this...'

'Listen,' said Cam. 'Do you think we should head back to the camp and follow the news properly? Maybe we could continue our investigation tomorrow, in daylight?'

'No!' answered both Iago and Renny, in perfect harmony.

'Didn't think you would,' grinned Cam.

'Might as well do something anyway,' said Iago, pulling down the peak of Renny's hat affectionately.

'Oi!' exclaimed Renny, fixing it in place.

Aretha stepped forward, and to my surprise, I saw the devious dog just behind her right leg, as if attached by an invisible string. He kept his head down. The sight of him made me smile – he was such a character.

'How did he get here?' I asked.

Looking down at him, Aretha said, 'Oh – he just followed us. He's lonely. He needs some friends.'

She bent down, patting him gently on the head and he whimpered softly in response. He'd found a friend in Aretha.

'C'mon then – let's get moving,' said Cam, pulling

Renny forward.

I joined Aretha, leaving Iago and Charlie alone together, bringing up the rear.

'You OK?' I heard him ask.

I looked back at them. Charlie glanced out at him from behind her hair and smiled.

In the moonlight, we picked our way carefully through the denser brush land on the edge of the open heath. Gradually, mounds of brambles and nettles gave way to a small wood on our right. Ahead of us, between the strange lights and our position, the ground was almost completely covered with nettles. The only things growing in between the nettles, as far as we could see, were clumps of thistles and the occasional bramble bush.

'Great!' sighed Charlie, as she and Iago came up behind me.

'Doesn't look too inviting,' said Cam, ruffling my hair.

'Maybe we should try going through this wood and look for a better route on the other side,' said Iago. 'Let's be careful though! If that guy we saw is anywhere, he'll be in there.'

'Why do you say that?' whispered Aretha, looking around nervously.

The dog whimpered slightly by her side, echoing her feelings.

'Because there's no need to patrol *that* area,' replied Iago, pointing to the nettle field. 'No one would go through that!'

He was right. We approached the wood quietly. Iago resumed his forward position, and Cam swept protectively behind Aretha and me. Charlie stayed just to our right and Renny flitted through the trees to our left, doing his best commando impression. There were no well-worn trails to follow; only the faint tracks the deer took between the trees.

Moving slowly forward, with only the moonlight to guide us, it took longer than we expected to make it through the small stretch of wood.

'Ow!' yelped Renny, stumbling over a root.

My heart leapt.

'Shhhh!' said Iago, helping him to his feet.

Even the dog growled softly at him. We stayed put for a few minutes afterwards, just in case anyone had heard him. Nothing happened, no sound of movement anywhere. Still we moved cautiously. Up ahead, the wood seemed to be thinning out a little. I hoped we were getting closer to the edge. I didn't like being in a dark wood, late at night.

A twig snapping somewhere to my left startled me so much I squealed like a pig.

Renny – instantly dropping to the ground, like a trained soldier – shushed me. Then the loud hoot of an owl burst through the silence. Renny gasped, but managed to cover his mouth to block any sound. A squeaking noise followed – a female owl answering her mate. Her shrill cry echoed through the still wood, sending a shivering sensation across my shoulders. My muscles tensed automatically.

I looked at Aretha and saw my fear mirrored in her face. Gripping her hand tightly in mine, I squeezed it. Charlie moved in from her post and took Aretha's other hand.

The three of us moved forward followed by Renny, who was now back on his feet, then Iago. Cam was still there somewhere behind us, although I only caught glimpses of him now and then, when a shaft of moonlight washed over him as he crept forward.

Suddenly, the dog rushed ahead and stared at something unseen. His white teeth shining in the moonlight, he began a deep-throated growl that stopped us dead. Had he turned into some evil were-dog, transformed by the moon?

'Shhhh, boy,' whispered Aretha, inching forward, her hand outstretched.

His growling grew louder and he drew his lips back farther, baring his canines. Aretha stopped, frightened by his hostile response. Iago stepped forward and stood full-square in front of the hound.

'I knew we shouldn't have let him come along,' he whispered angrily.

The dog lowered his head, knowing he was in trouble. Whining, he returned obediently to Aretha's side.

'I think he was trying to tell us something,' said Cam, who had come forward to see what the hold-up was.

'Yes,' I agreed. 'Maybe there's danger ahead?'

Bending down so that he was eye level with the dog, Iago whispered, 'Consider us warned, Dog, but next time, can you be a bit more subtle, please?'

He patted the dog on the head, then stood up.

'Let's keep moving,' he said.

We finally reached the edge of the wood. As we stood sheltered behind the last row of trees, we had our first clear view of the building that the strange lights came from. The blue-green hue was still visible, but from this position, it was much fainter than it had been from the stream. The building was long and wide, but no more than two storeys high. Its flat roof overhung the sides of the building.

'Strange,' said Renny. 'You'd expect the lights to get brighter the closer you got.'

'I know why,' said Cam.

'Why?' whispered Charlie.

'We're looking down on the building. Can't you see – the building is virtually underground. This wood must have a small gradual incline, so we're actually above it now.'

'Yes...' said Iago, joining in. 'The only place you can really see the lights from is the stream near our camp, because the heath runs flat all the way from there to here.'

'So,' I interrupted, 'the building is invisible from all other angles apart from the stream near where we camped.'

'What luck,' said Aretha.

'That's why they sent someone round to check on us,' mused Renny. 'They knew we'd be able to see them.'

'So – they *must be* up to something in there then!' said Charlie.

'That's a pretty giant leap, Charl',' answered Iago.

'After our last adventure, I think it's just one small step!'

She chuckled at her moon-landing joke and soon we all joined in, including Iago.

10

Renny sat down suddenly, getting out his laptop.
'I think we should check out what's supposed to be going on in that building,' he said.

'I still say they're just growing salad stuff,' said Cam.

'I looked for all documents with these coordinates,' said Renny, without lifting his head. 'I've found a planning application on the local council's website. And it seems you're right Cam – it's an application for a hydroponics plant.'

'See, I told you so,' said Cam.

'But – what about the creepy guard?' asked Charlie. 'Why would they send someone to our campsite to scare us?'

'I think you're right, Charlie,' said Renny. 'Something tells me that this is a little more than the hydroponics facility it claims to be. Course, I could be wrong, but I still say we should check it out!'

'Agreed,' said Iago and he and Cam crept right to the edge of the wood.

Just as they reached the outermost tree, lights flickered somewhere to the left of the building. It was a car approaching along the track that led to the facility. Cam and Iago stepped back into the cover of the trees.

I couldn't help being nosy, so I tiptoed up to join them.

The car – a jeep – pulled up outside the main entrance of the building and four men got out. I couldn't see clearly, but they were all big men, dressed completely in black. Two of them went to the back of the car and lifted out something. Holding one end each, their heavy boots crunched over the gravel as they made their way inside the building.

'Don't know who they were,' whispered Iago as we rejoined the others. 'But they don't look like ordinary security guards.'

'And what were they carrying?' asked Charlie.

'I don't know,' answered Iago, 'but this doesn't look right to me.'

He went to the edge of the wood again.

'Me either,' said Cam.

After watching the building for further signs of movement, Iago motioned Cam over. Their heads bobbed together in conversation for a few seconds before Cam came back to where Aretha and I, and the dog, were waiting.

'OK – you two hang back here. Iago and I will go check out the front of the building. Renny and Charlie will circle round the back, just to see what's there. If, and I mean only *if*, you get a signal from me that it's safe, you follow us in. Understood?'

'Yes Cam,' I said. 'As usual, *we* don't get to have *any* fun!'

'But we'll be scared if you all go and leave us here alone!' said Aretha quietly.

'Speak for yourself!' I said.

'You've got the dog,' said Cam, smiling at Aretha.

I sighed. I hate being treated like a baby.

'Anyway – how are you planning to get in?' I said. 'I mean, if they've got security guards, I'm sure they've got locks on their doors.'

Renny held out a memory stick.

'There's an app for that!' he said, and with a wink, he plugged the memory stick into his smartphone.

'No way!' said Charlie.

'It can't be legal,' added Cam.

'Who said anything about legal?' grinned Renny. 'Anyway, as far as I'm aware, breaking and entering isn't legal either.'

I looked at Iago, who'd come back to join us.

'Renny,' he said, 'make sure your phone's on vibrate.'

'Aw hey – you already checked that,' moaned Renny. 'Why didn't you double-check with everyone else?'

'Obvious reasons,' grinned Iago. 'OK – let's go.'

He walked away and Cam followed closely behind him.

'Tara – can you hold on to the laptop?' asked Renny.

'Sure,' I answered. 'Be careful.'

'I will,' he said. 'Oh – and keep me posted on any webcasts or other updates,' he added.

With a flurry of hand signals, Charlie and Renny set off along the edge of the wood, towards the back of the building. They moved silently, which was amazing considering Renny's ability to trip over anything more than one millimetre high. In the pale moonlight, we lost sight of them after a while. I began to feel slightly nervous, even though I knew that I would see them again in a few minutes. They'd have to leave the cover of the woods eventually and cross the open space around the building.

A very quiet ping alerted me to one of the sites Renny was keeping an eye on. He had so many pages open that I had to trawl through them searching for the one that had pinged. After a while, I figured out that it was the 'audioBoo' page that had updated. I could see that the update came from the BBC reporter at the scene of the G20 crisis site. I wanted to know what had happened, so I inserted his Bluetooth earpiece, clicking the message at the same time.

'Tragic news here at the site of the G20 summit. The illness that affected all of the members of today's G20 meeting has claimed its first victim. It has been confirmed that one of the world leaders has died of the illness. We have no information yet as to the identity of the individual. Speculation is rife here, and we have been promised a statement in the next hour...'

My stomach churned. Could it be the US President who had died? Swallowing hard, I pulled the earpiece out and turned to Aretha, who'd been watching me.

'What is it?' she whispered.

'I... I... can't believe it!' I answered. 'One of them has died!'

'Do you mean – one of the G20?'

'Yes! But they didn't say which one.'

'Oh, this is serious,' she said. 'We should tell the others.'

'We can't now,' I answered. 'They've gone.'

'We could phone them,' said Aretha.

'No,' I answered, suddenly seeing a way to be

involved in the adventure. 'We should follow them.'

Aretha looked at me. She could have questioned my logic, but she didn't. I think she was a tiny bit excited about joining in the adventure too.

'Well, all right, but we just go there, tell them, then leave,' she said.

Closing up the laptop, I replaced it securely in Renny's rucksack.

'There they are,' said Aretha, pointing into the distance.

Following her finger, I could just see two shadowy figures flitting across the open ground. Although it only took about five seconds for them to get across, I hoped that no one else was looking. They were quiet and fast, but they *were* visible.

As they disappeared into the shadow of the building, Aretha and the dog paced up and down.

I couldn't stop thinking about that news report. Which one of them had died? My mind raced through recent photos I had seen – twenty smiling, suited men and women, all trying to make the world work.

It can't be easy. I mean would you want to try to run this world? Keep everyone happy, and fed, and safe, and warm? Deal with every conflict? Try to find solutions to every problem? Stop people from destroying the planet, while allowing people freedom and the right to use resources? I wouldn't!

'Any sign of Cam or Iago?' Aretha asked, bringing me back to reality. 'What's keeping them?'

'Look, there they are!' I said.

Two shapes were moving towards the side of the building, away from the front entrance.

'Must've had word from Charlie and Renny. Maybe they've found a way in through the back,' I said.

'Probably not the best idea to try and sneak in through the front door,' said Aretha.

'Aretha,' I said, 'I don't care what Iago and Cam said – I'm not staying out here. They're probably going to have another adventure in there and we're sitting out here, twiddling our thumbs. Well! I'm not doing it. *Not* this time!'

Aretha's face froze.

'But what if it's dangerous?' she said. 'I mean – you don't go sneaking into some strange facility and expect a warm welcome, do you?'

'Don't let life pass you by, girl.' I replied. '*Carpe diem*!'

'What on earth does that mean?'

'It's Latin,' I told her. 'I saw it in a film called *Dead Poets Society*. It means "Seize the day".'

'Oh, I like it,' she said. '*Carpe diem*.' Then she turned to me and smiled. 'OK – let's do it!'

'Yes!' I replied, pleased to have a sidekick.

Boy would we be in trouble when Iago and Cam saw us.

11

Gathering our stuff and everyone else's – well, Renny's mostly – we crept carefully forward. His bag was cutting into my shoulder. I think he really did bring the kitchen sink.

Stopping after a while, we squatted down, so we could check for any sign of movement. The low heather bushes didn't provide much cover. We stayed still, listening carefully, scanning the horizon.

'Let's keep moving,' I whispered.

'Shouldn't we follow Renny and Charlie?' asked Aretha.

'No. We should take the quickest route. That way will take too long.'

I began to creep forward through the nettles, my cousin close behind me. We quickened our pace, crouching as we neared the clearing to the side of the low building. The blue light streamed from the windows at the front of the building. A dull throbbing sound accompanied it. It sounded like some kind of generator. Probably *was* just a hydroponics factory. We'd probably find row upon row of cucumbers being tricked into growing day and night by some state-of-the-art lighting rig. Those guys carrying that thing into the building might have just been technicians, even if they did look a bit like commandos.

Feeling braver now, I stood up straight. Aretha did the same. Tiptoeing silently forward, we crossed the open stretch of ground. It seemed to take forever.

Once safely in the shade of the building's overhanging roof, I breathed a huge sigh of relief.

'Stage one done – not captured yet,' I whispered.

Aretha smiled, her eyes sparkling with excitement. I think she was enjoying this as much as I was, no matter what she said about being scared. Something moved near her feet, startling me. I jumped.

'It's only the dog, silly!' she said.

'I'd forgotten all about him,' I replied.

As if he knew we were talking about him, he peeked his nose around Aretha's leg cautiously. He was definitely *her* dog. She was going to find it hard when she had to give him back to the old lady.

'OK, let's carry on,' I said.

We began moving carefully along the side of the building. We tiptoed soundlessly towards the back, the dog sticking close to Aretha. I made a mental note to remind myself that we had a dog in tow – I didn't need any more heart-stopping moments.

Reaching the corner, I stopped and drew in a couple of breaths. I needed to calm down. When I felt ready, I peeped around the corner.

Nothing!

Well nothing scary anyway.

Turning back, I shared the news with my cousin.

'Phhheewww!' she said.

'What do you mean?' I asked.

'Well,' she said. 'I don't *really* want to go in there.'

'But, I thought you were enjoying this?'

'Well – I am, kind of!'

'What do you mean – *kind of*?'

'Well – I'm fine with all this creeping around in the moonlight. I just don't want to go in there.'

'Why not?'

'I just don't want to go in, that's all,' she said, and I could see her chin go up stubbornly.

'Well – I'm not staying out here either,' I answered.

'I don't expect you to,' she replied. 'In fact, I don't need you to.'

I thought she might be angry with me, but she wasn't. She seemed calm.

'I've got company,' she said, patting the dog on the head.

He wagged his tail, obviously enjoying the attention. I knew she was right – he was more protection to her than I was. But I still felt bad even thinking about leaving her outside on her own. Iago's instructions to stay put until called came back to me, but I was too curious now to turn away.

'I don't mind if you go, honestly,' she said. 'Besides, someone *should* stay on the outside. Imagine if you lot are all caught by those security guards for trespassing. Might be good to have someone on the outside to call the police. I bet I end up coming to your rescue before the night is over.'

'Not very likely,' I said. 'You sure you'll be OK?'

She nodded.

I put my rucksack on my back and picked up Renny's. Still feeling a bit guilty, I hugged my cousin, then headed around the corner. There was a dark outline jutting out from the flat wall. It was long and straight, but narrow. It looked like a door that had been left ajar. Apart from the door, the rest of the building was featureless brick. Making sure I kept to the shadows, I tiptoed towards it. I listened for any trace of the others, but couldn't hear anything.

When I reached the door, I saw that I'd been right – it was slightly ajar. There was a piece of wood wedged in the opening. Renny must have left it like that. I suppose that was sensible. If they needed to make a quick getaway, it was probably better not to have to fumble around with his break-in app.

What was I going to do? Should I just walk straight in? Should I call out to the others first? Should I try phoning one of them? I didn't know the answer, so I decided to do the first. I would just walk straight in.

Gripping the door handle, I readied myself. *Just pull it and walk straight through!* That was easier said than done. *On a count of three then...*

One.

Two.

Three...

Pumped with adrenaline, I tugged harder than I needed to and the door flew open, its hinges squeaking loudly. I winced.

Looking to my right, I could see Aretha's cross face peeking around the corner. Even my younger cousin was annoyed with me. I could only imagine how furious the others would be, if they'd heard me.

I felt something grab my arm suddenly, dragging me inside the door. In the total darkness, I couldn't make anything out and before I knew it, I was pinned against the back wall. My heart pounded and I squeezed my eyes shut in fear.

A faint light came through my eyelids and as I opened my eyes, the torch that had been trained on me, illuminated the face of my captor. It was Iago, his normally handsome face set in an angry frown. To be honest, at that moment, I'd have preferred if the horrible security guard had captured me.

'What are you doing here?' Iago asked.

'I... I...'

My tongue stuck to the roof of my mouth as all the moisture disappeared.

'You were told to stay put! Can't you follow a simple instruction? And where's Aretha?'

'Sh... she's outside,' I said.

'What?' It was more of a statement than a question. 'You left my little sister out there, on her own!'

I couldn't have felt worse if I'd thrown up on his shoes!

Taking his phone from his pocket, Iago tapped out a short message.

'She's got the dog with her,' I squeaked.

That only seemed to make him worse. Muttering under his breath, he put his head in his hands and sighed. He was really annoyed.

Charlie appeared from out of nowhere, like a good fairy.

'Iago,' she said sternly, 'calm down. Aretha will be fine.' Then, turning to me, she asked, 'Why didn't you bring her with you?'

'She didn't want to come in.'

I felt like crying now. I felt like running away and hiding with Aretha in the safety of the outdoors. I felt that any place would be better than this.

Iago checked his phone for messages.

'Aretha's fine and she wants to stay outside.'

Charlie whispered something in his ear, and he smiled.

Then he turned to me and said, 'Right, you can stay, but the first sign of danger – you're out of here. This seems to be just a huge warehouse, so we're going to check the rest of the building.'

Thanks Charl', I thought. I looked up, taking in my surroundings. The ceiling was high; the empty shelves reaching up towards it like a giant ladder.

Charlie put her arm around my shoulders, squeezing me. I hugged back in response. I felt happier now.

Unfortunately, the happiness was fleeting because as soon as my brother saw me coming round the corner of the high shelving units, his face turned to stone. I was *not* in the mood for a repeat performance. I would defend myself this time. I stepped forward, ready to face the Wrath of Cam.

'Why didn't you stay outside?' he started.

'We've already been through this, Cam,' said Iago. 'Just leave it.'

Cam wrinkled his nose but he kept quiet.

'Oi! What's *she* doing here?' came a voice from the corner of the big warehouse.

'Shut up Renny,' we all replied together.

'What did *I* do?' asked Renny.

Cam groaned.

Renny looked at me. 'Oh good, you've got my bag.

Did you bring the laptop?'

'Course I did,' I replied.

I passed him the rucksack and watched him pull out the computer.

'Oh!' I said, suddenly remembering my news. 'One of the G20 leaders is dead!'

'Make that two!' said Renny, turning the laptop to face us.

The BBC webpage headline read, 'Another leader dies!'

'Oh no!' said Charlie, her hands flying up to her mouth.

'Aretha thinks we should head back to camp and follow the news there,' I said, turning to look at the others. 'I mean, this is pretty major news. Aretha wanted to come and get you. She just backed out in the end. She didn't like the idea of getting trapped in here. What do you think? Should we leave?'

A door banging stopped anyone from answering my question. It didn't sound like it was the door to this room. Still – instinct made me crouch down. When I looked around, I saw that the others had done the same. Renny was closing his laptop, since the glow from the screen was sure to give away his position. I was expecting footsteps, so my ears strained. I looked at Cam – he was motionless, and seemed to be listening too.

A tiny glow of light from Iago's phone illuminated Charlie's face.

'Where do you think that came from?' she mouthed.

He shrugged his shoulders and reached out his hand. She squeezed it.

Cam was the first to move, crawling forward through

the rows of shelving, towards a large metal door set into the inner wall of the warehouse. Stuffing the laptop into his rucksack, Renny followed. Iago and Charlie crept forward as one, and I moved last. Now, I wasn't so sure I wanted to be in here. Maybe Aretha had been right to stay outside. This place was creepy.

12

Cam pulled back the large bolts in the metal door. A dim light flickered in a corridor just beyond the warehouse we were in. Peeping carefully around the doorpost, he checked the corridor for signs of movement. Turning back to face us, he shook his head. There didn't appear to be anyone out there.

Cam stepped around the door into the corridor, with Renny shadowing his every move. It was quite cute seeing Renny trying to be as brave as his big brother. He just *so* didn't cut it! Charlie followed, and Iago waited until I had passed him before entering the hallway.

'Which way?' whispered Renny.

Cam raised his finger to his lips, and then pointed towards one end of the corridor. As we all stood there silently, a faint noise drifted down towards us. It was the tinny sound of a cheap portable television. I guessed there was a security office somewhere in that direction.

Cam signalled that we should head the opposite way. Iago nodded his dark head in agreement. Gripping my arm in one hand, he held the other out for Charlie to take. She smiled at him, and took it. Then she rested her head on his shoulder, just for a second. As he moved off towards the other end of the corridor, I shrugged my arm free of his. I didn't need to be dragged along. I could find my own way!

I followed my cousin noiselessly along the corridor. We passed several doors, then Iago stopped and opened one. The rest of us lined up against the wall as he checked inside. After a few seconds, he closed it and shrugged his shoulders. Can't have been very interesting.

We continued on down the corridor towards some more doors at the end. For some reason, one of these seemed interesting to Iago. Then I saw the keypad to the right of the lock. Ah! Now I understood. If there was anything interesting at this facility, it would be kept in a secure room. I still wasn't sure that this place was anything more than a hydroponics facility. But why the security guard, and those men in the jeep, then?

Iago signalled Renny forward. Taking out his phone, Renny scrolled through his apps until he found the right one. He placed the phone next to the security panel and ran the app. I couldn't see the screen but within a matter of seconds, the security light changed from red to green.

Iago tried the door handle. We waited. I was expecting alarm bells, or sirens, or flashing lights. Thankfully, nothing happened and Iago stepped inside, the rest of us following as quickly and quietly as we could.

The light was very dim but even from my position at the back, I could see the strange blue-green hue we had seen from across the heath. *This must be the hydroponics room.* We were going to be so disappointed if it really was filled with rows of cucumbers.

Iago closed the door quietly behind us. We were in another large, high-ceilinged room.

'Strange,' I whispered to Renny. 'It seems to be quite

bright in here, but I can hardly make out anything.'

'It's the colour of the light,' replied Renny. 'It's a really narrow bandwidth. It means that very little light is reflected. We can only see reflected light. Do you understand?'

I didn't really, but I nodded anyway. This really wasn't the time for one of Renny's science lectures.

As my eyes adjusted to the weird light, I could just make out something up ahead. 'What's that?' I asked.

I could only see the object if I looked slightly to the left of it. For some reason, if I looked straight on, I lost sight of it.

'Where?' asked Renny.

'Here,' I said, feeling my way forwards, my arms stretched out in front.

As I reached it, I tried to focus. I had to blink several times before I could believe my eyes.

I was looking at a small rodent. It was strapped inside a kind of capsule – a metal oval, with a large Perspex window in the front. Its paws were pinned back, held by tiny straps. The rodent – let's just call it a rat – didn't move, but I could see that it was conscious because its piercing eyes followed my movements. Looking to the left of it, I could see capsule after capsule.

In disbelief, I walked past the first capsule, to the second. Sure enough, the next capsule contained an identical rat, in identical conditions. I'd heard of animal testing and I knew that using lab-rats had led to major medical discoveries. I still though it was horrible. But this seemed somehow cruel – the way these animals were being treated, their legs pinned back, their frightened eyes. There was no concern for their welfare. They were like prisoners. Then Charlie's loud gasp told me that she'd made the same gruesome discovery.

I walked towards where I'd heard Charlie's voice. When I got there, Iago was already by her side, comforting her. She was leaning against him, sobbing quietly. I knew that Charlie loved animals, but I couldn't imagine her being that upset by imprisoned rats. I mean, yes – they were being held, clearly against their will. It made me feel sick, but I couldn't understand Charlie's reaction.

I was on the verge of saying so, when Renny patted Charlie on the shoulder saying, 'Don't worry Charl', we'll get them out!'

Him too! What on earth was going on?

Edging past Iago and Charlie, I scrunched up my eyes to try and see better. I needn't have done. The blinding glare from Renny's LED torch illuminated what Charlie had reacted so strongly to. There – strapped in exactly the same position as the rat, was a dog. My knees went weak.

There were a few things about the dog that made my stomach lurch. Firstly, the fact that it was a dog – an animal people usually kept as a pet – clearly being used for experiments. Secondly, the dog looked exactly like the one that was sitting outside with Aretha, down to the startlingly blue eyes. And finally, it was obviously in pain. Soundproof though its prison capsule was, I could see its mouth moving as it writhed.

'I have to do something,' sobbed Charlie, lifting her head off Iago's chest. 'We can't just leave them here, like this!'

'But... we can't just release them all, Charlie,' said

Iago softly. 'They could be dangerous. They're definitely going to be angry and aggressive. And anyway, they probably don't know how to look after themselves.'

'Besides, can you imagine how popular we'd be round here, if we released all those rats,' said Renny, pointing to where I'd just been.

'And... we don't know what they might have been injected with,' added Cam.

'But look at him,' cried Charlie, running her hand along the glass at the front of the capsule. 'Just let me help *him*, please?'

Tears brimmed over the edges of her lashes, leaving long wet streaks down her tanned face. She lowered her head.

Iago cleared his throat. 'Maybe we could *just* take a look at him.'

Charlie brightened instantly.

'I don't think you should,' cautioned Cam.

'Well, I do!' answered Iago.

'I just think we should be careful,' replied Cam.

'Look at the poor thing,' said Iago. 'He's clearly in pain.'

'I agree that this is all truly horrible,' said Cam. 'But we should think this through before we act.'

'But he needs our help,' said Charlie. 'Please Iago?'

Stepping in front of the capsule, Iago gripped a handle at its side. A sharp hiss, as the air within the capsule was released, indicated that he'd gone ahead and done it.

Charlie reached out, pulling the glass cover open slowly. All the while, she whispered soothingly at the poor creature inside. It had stopped writhing and made no sound as she reached her hand inside the capsule. Its eyes darted around, puzzled, as if it didn't understand what was happening.

Its frightened response to Charlie's care made me think that it had never been treated with any kindness, so it didn't recognise it. I thought of Aretha's devious dog; he had clearly been mistreated in the past. Had he come from here too? Now I began to see him in a new light. He was still devious, but maybe he had his reasons.

Watching Charlie's careful movements, I began to think that maybe Iago had been right. We couldn't save *all* these animals – not right now anyway. But we could try to help some of them.

Slowly, Charlie undid the first restraint. The dog showed no sign of movement. Its paw remained fixed where it was. I felt a lump start to swell in my throat; the dog didn't even know how to move its paw. Or had he been there so long that his muscles didn't work any more, and he couldn't move it?

'C'mon boy,' said Charlie gently. 'It's all right.'

The dog whimpered softly, just a tiny short whimper, but a response at least. Charlie flashed an excited smile at us. Then she reached in to release the second restraint.

The dog's lightening movement took us all by surprise. I had never seen a creature act so fast in my life. In less than the blink of an eye, the paralysed paw flew forward. Its claws tore into Charlie's arm.

Shrieking in pain, Charlie jumped back, falling to the ground. Iago slammed the door of the dog's capsule shut. The tortured creature scratched at the glass with its free paw. The terrible squeaking, like chalk on a board, tore through my nerves, making my teeth hurt.

'I'm so sorry. I'm so sorry,' was all Iago kept saying,

as he knelt beside Charlie.

Blood oozed from the three gashes on her arm. The dog's claws had never been worn down by walking, so they were as sharp as a cat's. Charlie just sat there, staring at her arm – her face suddenly pale from the shock.

Realising that I was in charge of the medical kit, I sprang into action. Digging through the contents, I handed Iago the spray-on disinfectant and wound cleaner. I opened a package of sterile gauze bandage, which he took and wrapped gently around Charlie's arm.

'Do you want a painkiller?' I asked.

Charlie just shook her head.

'What made him do that?' she asked.

'Listen Charl',' answered Iago, 'he didn't know that you were trying to help him. Maybe, in his life, he's only ever been mistreated by humans. He doesn't know that you're different. He probably just acted on instinct. And his instincts told him that this might be a chance to escape. You'd have probably done the same.'

'Yeah – I suppose so,' sighed Charlie.

'Are you OK?' I asked.

'It was just such a shock. I'll be OK.' she said.

'Guys..?' whispered Renny. 'Come take a look!'

He had his laptop open and was watching a live stream from Evan Andrews – the Africa correspondent we had seen in Somalia earlier.

'Turn the volume up a little bit,' said Iago. 'This room seems pretty well sealed. I don't think we need to worry about being heard, unless someone's standing right outside the door.'

We gathered around Renny. The scenes were horrific. There were bodies everywhere. It was as if people had just dropped dead mid-step.

Andrews was standing in a marketplace where mounds of fruits, vegetables, spices, and meat were all laid out on tables. The stallholders lay slumped over their produce, their customers on the ground in front of the stalls.

Andrews looked directly into the camera, tears welling at the corners of his blue eyes.

'I've never seen anything like this before. I mean, they're all dead – every single one of them. When I arrived here less than an hour ago, they were all alive. This was a normal busy market day. We only came here to stock up on supplies. There hadn't been any reports of the virus this far west so we decided to investigate why. I just don't know what's going on...'

His shoulders began shaking and he lowered his eyes.

Then the image cut out.

13

We all stood there for a few moments. The scenes we had just witnessed kept playing over and over in my head. I felt sorry for Andrews, but not as sorry as I did for those poor people. They had all just been cut down by some hideous entity that wasn't even big enough to form a cell of its own – it just invaded the cells of others. I really *hate* viruses.

'I've never heard of anything that can act that fast,' Renny said.

'Yeah, surely it takes time for a virus to infest cells?' added Cam.

'So this isn't possible?' asked Iago.

'Well, just because something hasn't happened before doesn't mean it never will,' replied Renny. 'Viruses mutate all the time. They even pick up bits of DNA from their hosts – that's why we have swine flu and bird flu. They're like ticking time bombs, becoming smarter and smarter with each infection. Their goal in life is to survive. Their motto is *"Adapt"*. Did you know that viruses are probably the oldest organisms on earth?'

'Ugghh!' I shuddered, disgusted.

'Iago?' came Charlie's voice from behind us.

She was still sitting where we'd left her. I thought

she'd been watching the report with us. Her voice sounded strange, kind of weak and broken. But that was nothing compared to the sight of her.

Her face was not just pale, but had taken on a greenish hue. It might have been the lights, but whatever it was, she looked awful. Her lips looked bluish as well and beads of sweat formed on her forehead.

'CHARLIE!' cried Iago, skidding down beside her. *'What happened?'*

'I don't know,' she coughed. 'I... I... just don't feel well.'

'Do you think it has anything to do with the dog scratching her?' I asked.

'He could be carrying something toxic,' replied Renny.

Iago checked her pulse and felt her forehead.

'She's burning up! We've got to get her to a hospital. Whatever these monsters are doing in here – whatever poison they are testing on these animals, Charlie's become infected. She needs medical help.'

He reached down and scooped Charlie up in his arms, holding her close to him. Limply, she looped her arms around his neck. She tried to smile at him, but the effort made her close her eyes. She was getting weaker by the minute. I'd never seen anyone get so sick, so fast. I'd heard the doctor once explaining to Mum that meningitis can cause the patient to go downhill really quickly. What if she had something like that? Would we be able to get her to a hospital in time?

We raced for the door, passing the rows of capsules. Iago didn't care how much noise he made now. I think he would have fought a giant yeti if it had crossed his path.

Cam reached the door first and opened it carefully. The corridor must have been empty because he didn't hesitate. We followed him. I had to shield my eyes from the light. Even though the bulbs in the corridor were dim, the sudden change in light was very painful.

Before my eyes had adjusted fully, I felt my phone vibrate. Reaching into my pocket, I pulled it out as quickly as I could. I knew it could only be from one person. And I knew that she wouldn't have sent a message unless she absolutely had to.

I had to slow down to read the message, my eyes still not used to the brightness. The text simply read: Get out now!

I stared at my phone as if it could tell me more. What did she mean? Whatever it was, she didn't need to worry – we were on our way out anyway.

Then the message became suddenly horribly clear. At the end of the corridor by the main foyer two black clad men appeared – probably the same guys from the jeep. I knew this wasn't good. Big men dressed in black usually mean business. They stopped in front of the reception desk, their backs to us.

Cam, who was in front, slowed, but didn't stop. The door to the warehouse – our only means of escape – was between those men and us.

Cam and Iago made it through the door before the men turned. Renny and I, on the other hand were just far enough behind to get caught trying. What would Cam and Iago do? Would they just leave us here to fend for ourselves?

I could see Iago handing over Charlie gently, then

whispering something in Cam's ear. He bent his head and kissed Charlie on the forehead. Her eyes flickered just a little, but they didn't open. Wherever she was, she was too weak to come back from it. Iago stepped back into the hallway, letting the door slam shut.

I stopped mid-step and Renny slammed into my back.

'Owww!' I shouted, instinctively.

'Sorry, but how could I have known...' he began, and then stopped.

Iago's broad back was now between the men and me, and I was glad for once that I was small. I felt protected by my much bigger cousin. I was hugely relieved that he had decided not to leave Renny and I all alone to face the music. He could have escaped with Cam. Then I realised that Iago had to stay behind, if he wanted Cam to have any chance of escaping with Charlie. If he'd left Renny and I to face the music on our own we'd have blabbed. Not intentionally, but we'd never hold up under interrogation.

Creeping right up behind my cousin, I gripped the back of his shirt. He moved his arm behind his back and I grabbed his hand. My legs trembled and cold beads of sweat formed just below my hairline. I could hear Renny fidgeting in the background, like he always did when he was nervous. I turned my head to comfort him, but the words froze on my tongue.

Two men were coming up the centre of the corridor behind us, flanked by two more black-clad men. Now that I could see them up close, I had no doubt they were security guards. The group came from the direction we'd just been. They must have been in the other room – the one we hadn't had time to check out.

The man on the left was pretty ordinary. He was of average height, medium build, wearing normal clothes, and in fact, had nothing remarkable, or even interesting, about him at all. He could have been any guy you pass in the street.

The man on the right was tall, silver-haired and expensively dressed. His fine wool overcoat was definitely 'designer' and his tanned face most likely the result of summers spent in Cannes, or some Caribbean paradise. He was probably more than fifty, but he looked like he kept himself fit. When he flashed a smile at me, his teeth were Hollywood white and perfectly straight.

Renny now backed up into me, holding his rucksack in front of him like a shield.

Tapping Iago lightly on the back, I whispered, 'Turn around.'

Without shifting his weight, Iago turned his head. Immediately he swung round in an arc, Renny and I moving with him as though we were attached.

Mr Hollywood-Whites waved his hand, laughing disarmingly.

'Do not be frightened, children.' He spoke in heavily accented English. 'You won't come to any harm, although you really shouldn't break into private establishments in the middle of the night!'

Although his words were not threatening, the tone of his voice carried venom. Underneath all his expensive clothes and grooming, this man was a snake. I shrank back in fear and I grabbed Iago's hand again. He squeezed mine. So – the bad vibes could be felt by everyone then.

Apparently not!

Renny, for some reason, stepped forward and decided to do the talking.

Some people are good at thinking on their feet. Renny is definitely not. His talents lie in the behind-the-scenes department. Under pressure, he's rubbish – he starts to babble.

'Um... we didn't see anything – honest! We... we were just—'

'Renny!' shouted Iago.

Great! Now they *knew* that we *had* seen something.

Renny decided, wisely, that he should keep his mouth shut. Whimpering slightly, he returned to his position behind Iago's back. He looked at me sheepishly.

'Oh, well, if you didn't see anything then you're free to go,' Mr Hollywood-Whites said.

He swept his arm in the direction of the front entrance and Renny moved to step towards it. I rammed my heel into his toe. He got the message.

'On the other hand – if you *did* see something, we might have a little problem.'

The man stared hard at us, his unsettling gaze moving from one to the other. When he smiled, his face changed, but his hard eyes didn't.

'Let's just go somewhere and have a little chat, shall we?' he said.

A large hand mauled my shoulder, dragging me away from Iago. My legs weakened as panic surged through me. My arms flailed hopelessly in his direction. But he couldn't help me – two of the security guards were hauling him backwards. He kicked his legs in protest, but they were too strong for him. Renny was in much the same situation as I was – it only took one of these huge men to hold him still. They dragged us back along the corridor, past the 'torture room' we'd just left. The guards pushed and pulled us as we struggled in vain. I knew that we couldn't escape, but instinct is strong.

Mr Hollywood-Whites entered a code into keypad by the door, next to the one with the animals in, and the guards dragged us in. The same low blue-green light filtered eerily around. It took a few seconds for my eyes to adjust again. When they did, I was horrified.

14

This room, like the other one, contained capsules. The difference was that these capsules were much, much bigger.

'Ah!' said Mr Hollywood-Whites. 'So you did take a tiny peek at our little friends next door. Don't be afraid to admit it – it's written all over your outraged faces.'

His mocking tone made my back stiffen. I stared hard ahead, avoiding his gaze.

He paced slowly back and forth in front of us, drumming his fingers together.

'So! Are you the adventurous campers my guard told me about earlier on?' he asked.

Even his questions could sound threatening. None of us uttered a word.

'Never mind,' Mr Hollywood-Whites said shrugging. 'Fortunately, I have room for a few overnight guests.'

What? Was he planning on locking us inside those capsules, like the animals next door?

The guard's grip on me had relaxed a little. Dropping down quickly, I was able to slip through his grasp. I made a run for it. I could escape and raise the alarm.

The guard recovered in time to grab my sleeve. He didn't stop me but the effect sent me reeling forward.

Stumbling, I tried to grab on to anything I could to steady myself. My hand grasped something hard and I clung on to it as tightly as I could.

I heard the same hissing sound we'd heard when Iago had opened the dog's capsule – only this time much, much louder. The door of the capsule flew open in my hand, doing nothing to break my fall. Landing painfully on the hard tiled floor, I juddered to a stop. Then I heard the sound.

It was just a tiny cough.

Sitting up, I looked from Renny to Iago. Had they heard the sound too? Both of them looked confused. It seemed they had.

The second cough was louder and more racking than the first, but it was the sound that came after it that was distinctly human.

It was a cry – *the cry of a child.*

Blood drummed in my head and I could feel my heartbeat quicken. Turning my head to the side, I dry heaved several times. I hadn't seen the inside of the capsule I had opened accidentally, but I didn't need to. I knew that the child inside this capsule was restrained in exactly the same way as the rat, and the dog next door.

These men were experimenting on children!

15

A million questions fired around my head, none of which I could answer at that moment. There was one question that kept springing back into my mind – *why?*

I stood up slowly, bracing myself for the horror.

I was looking into the face of a boy, probably ten years old. His skin was tanned and his fair hair was cut short. He didn't look as if he'd been harmed and although he was restrained, there were no tubes, or anything attached to him. But the look of terror in his blue eyes was more than I could bear.

Screeching like a banshee, I flung myself at the smaller man, who happened to be nearest to me at the time. Beating on his chest with my hands, I wailed, 'But why? Why would you do this to a child? Why?'

Mr Hollywood-Whites grabbed me, pulling me off his colleague.

Dusting down the front of his suit, he said, 'So far, all we've done to James is borrow a little bit of his blood. Luckily for him, the virus grew in his blood cells and we didn't have to inject him with it.'

I tried to understand what this man was saying to me, but it was just too horrendous for my brain to process.

They were using this imprisoned child's blood to grow a virus! Was that what he had said?

Two of the security guards grabbed me, lifting me off the ground so that my legs dangled like a rag doll's. I tried to lash out at one or the other, but I couldn't quite reach.

Out of the corner of my eye, I noticed that Iago had moved towards the capsule during my unplanned diversion. He was undoing the straps restraining the child. *Well done, Iago*. I needed to give him more time. Swinging my legs from side to side, I wailed again. I was beginning to annoy the two men holding me, but I didn't care. I was definitely causing a distraction.

Renny did the same. We managed to keep the guards busy for a few seconds. Then I heard a clicking sound.

I stopped struggling just before Renny did. The sound still rang in my ears. It was unfamiliar but at the same time, I knew what it was. As I looked around, I saw the shiny metal barrel pressed against Iago's temple.

His hands were still on the child's restraint, but they weren't moving now.

'Step away,' hissed Mr Hollywood-Whites.

Iago hesitated, just for a second, but then did as he'd been told. One of the security men stepped forward, and secured the restraint.

'What's going on here?' asked Iago.

Although his voice was quiet, I could hear the rage in it. Iago was holding his temper, but only just.

Mr Hollywood-Whites smiled cruelly.

'This...' he said, his arm sweeping in an arc, '...this is just the beginning!' He paused. 'Well, actually – what you saw next door was the beginning. This is... how should we call it? Phase two. Like I said, I just needed James' blood.'

'So let him go then!' I shouted.

'Oh – don't get on your high horse, Missy,' he laughed. 'I'll let him go, eventually.'

'What do you mean – *eventually*?' Iago asked.

'Once our work here is done, I'll let him go!'

'What work?' asked Renny, stepping out from behind Iago.

The look on my brother's face told me that he knew something. Stealing a glance at his hands, I could see the low light from his phone's screen. He had been checking something out. Maybe he'd been following the news. Renny lives with his Bluetooth permanently in his ear. He even falls asleep with it in sometimes.

'I think I've told you enough,' said Mr Hollywood-Whites. 'For now, let's just say that you are my guests. I was going to let you stay here, maybe keep James company.'

His brutal smile made me shiver. What company would we be for James, if we were all imprisoned in separate capsules?

'But I think it would be wiser to keep a closer eye on you three. Take them!' He waved his gun in the direction of the door.

The guards converged on us suddenly, taking our rucksacks from us. Renny just about had time to shove his phone in his pocket. I could see from his eyes that he had news to tell us.

Leaving the capsule room behind, I felt a mixture of guilt and anger. Guilt that I hadn't been able to free James, and anger at the monster who'd put him there in the first place.

The security guards dragged us to a lift near the building's entrance. Mr Hollywood-Whites pressed '1' and as I looked up, I could see that there was a mezzanine level above us.

We were shoved up against the back wall, and sandwiched in by the muscle-bound guards. You could almost smell the steroids oozing from their pores, or was that just body odour? I decided not to breathe for the rest of the journey.

Luckily for me, it didn't take long. The doors opened and the guards stepped out. Sucking in a couple of deep breaths, I felt the welcome surge of oxygen through my body.

'Why were you holding your breath, Tar'?' asked Iago.

'You don't know what it's like being small,' I huffed. 'My head is at armpit height. I just wish people would take more interest in personal hygiene.'

He wrinkled his nose in disgust.

Mr Hollywood-Whites must have been last into the lift since he was already heading towards a large door by the time enough bodies had shifted for me to see him. I couldn't see any sign of the other man.

First, Iago was jerked through the lift door by two of the guards. One of the others laid his hands on me next and I tried to shrug them off. I knew there was no point, but I was so angry about James.

He hauled me out onto a balcony, which overlooked the main entrance. Now I could see the reception desk with several other corridors leading away. The blue light we'd seen from outside, also flowed out of these corridors. I could just make out a row of plants through an open door. Maybe they really were running a hydroponics factory as a cover.

Renny was still leaning against the mirrored back wall of the lift, a faraway look in his eyes. He was probably still listening to something. The other guard stepped back into the lift. Raising his arms peacefully towards him, Renny said, 'Hey, Hey! It's OK – I won't fight.'

The guard grabbed him roughly all the same, and we were both dragged towards a large wooden door. Iago was already inside.

Glancing around, I could see that this was some kind of boardroom-cum-office-cum-communications centre. The long room had a row of short, wide windows along the top. Its white walls contained several huge screens; some displaying images, some documents. There was a long dark-wood boardroom table, with plush chairs and several thick rugs almost covering the floor.

The guards dragged some heavy office chairs forward, near to the boardroom table, and checked us over before shoving us down roughly. They found Renny's and Iago's phones and flung them onto the boardroom table. One of them set about tying our legs with rope, another saw to our hands. Our rucksacks were tossed into a corner. I flinched as I heard the crunch of collapsing metal. I hoped my iPad had survived. Renny's laptop, though his smallest, was one of those heavy duty reinforced ones, so it should have been OK.

Mr Hollywood-Whites was some way off in an office space, completely separated by glass walls from the rest of the room. Although the high desk and the laptop blocked most of him from view, I could still see his face – his hard mouth set in concentration.

'Come!' commanded Mr Hollywood-Whites without raising his head.

The security guards left us, hurrying to his office.

'Psssst,' whispered Renny.

'What?' answered Iago.

'The outbreak in Somalia...'

'Renny, this really isn't the time. We're trapped. We need to focus on right here, right now.'

'I agree,' said Renny. 'But I thought you'd like to know that the virus seems to have died out. Evan Andrews should have held on just a bit longer.'

'What do you mean, he should have held on?' Iago asked, frustrated. 'Held on to what?'

'He couldn't take it, so he packed his stuff and got the first flight out of there. But now the virus seems to have worn itself out. His story might have had a happier ending if he'd stuck around. Ironic – huh?'

'Yeah, too bad for him,' I answered, remembering the horrific scenes he'd witnessed.

'Why would the virus just stop though?' asked Iago.

'Because *we* designed it that way,' came a voice from near the door.

16

All three of us spun our heads towards the speaker. It was the other man we'd met earlier – the totally unremarkable one.

'You! But *why*?' asked Renny.

The man just hung his head.

'Let *me* explain,' came the chilling voice of Mr Hollywood-Whites as he walked towards us. 'You see, Dr Faible here is a genius when it comes to chromosomes and genes and all those little building blocks. However, he is not very good at business.'

Faible looked up at Mr Hollywood-Whites. He seemed frightened of him.

'Anyway,' continued his tormentor. 'I needed his special skills for my business.'

'What *sort* of business?' asked Iago, his top lip curling.

'You mean – you don't know who I am?' replied Mr Hollywood-Whites, looking slightly offended.

Iago looked at me. Shrugging my shoulders, I looked at Renny, who simply shook his head.

'Oh well, you *are* quite young. Maybe my name rings a bell – Peter Gek?'

Again, we all looked at each other blankly.

'Nope,' answered Iago.

Gek balled his fists and began pacing up and down in front of us. Then a forced calm look came over his face.

'You'll *never* forget my name after today,' he sneered, his hooded eyes gleaming.

'Why is that?' asked Iago.

'Because of this,' he announced triumphantly, opening his laptop and placing it on the end of the boardroom table nearest to us.

It was GGN24 – a streaming news channel. The perky blonde anchorwoman was talking over some scenes of ambulances, police cars and flashing cameras. The text at the bottom of the screen read: 'Live from the G20 summit venue'. We didn't need to hear the sound to know that we were looking at the outbreak site. Gek turned up the volume.

'*...the latest information we have is that the number of deaths now stands at four...*'

'FOUR?' I shouted, not believing my ears.

Iago shook his head and Renny stared at his shoes – he seemed to have noticed a speck of dirt and was trying to remove it.

Muting the volume, Gek laughed. 'Oh don't pretend they were heroes. They are just a bunch of power-hungry egomaniacs. Who else would want to be a politician?'

'That's no reason to kill them!' Iago answered.

'Believe me – that is *not* my reason,' he replied.

'What is?' asked Iago, very, very quietly.

Gek turned away from the screen, fixing Iago with a cold, hard stare.

'Let's come back to that – shall we?' He turned to face Dr Faible, his mouth curled in a sneer. 'As my friend here just implied – we've been quite busy. You see... the outbreaks in Somalia are our handiwork too.'

'You really did that?' I asked.

I just couldn't believe what I was hearing.

'I kept thinking that something didn't add up,' muttered Renny. 'That virus killed people too quickly.'

'Aha! You're right, young man. How very clever of you!'

'What do you mean, "too quickly"?' Iago asked Renny.

'If a virus kills its host too quickly, it dies along with the host,' Renny replied.

'What's a host?' I asked.

'A host is a body that the virus invades. The virus needs the host to stay alive long enough so that it can transfer to another host.'

'You mean – another body,' I said.

'But can't viruses live outside the body?' Iago asked. 'Isn't that why they have the "Catch it, kill it, bin it" posters everywhere?'

'Yes, it's true that most viruses can live outside the host body for a few hours,' answered Renny. 'But it needs to find a new host within a few hours or it just dies.'

Iago nodded, then asked, 'So – if this virus kills so quickly that it cannot transfer to another host – why didn't it just die out after the first outbreak?'

'Yes,' I joined in. 'If it killed everyone instantly there was no one left to carry it out of that village. So how did it get out?'

'Not everyone died!' said Renny quietly.

'But—' Iago began, and then stopped.

'Oh come on,' I said. 'What am *I* not seeing?'

Renny looked over at Gek, his brows furrowing. The horrible man just smirked back at him.

'The reporter,' said Renny.

Gek's sudden laughter frightened me and I saw Renny shrink back. Iago's face clouded over, his dark eyes angry.

'The reporter,' I said, finally understanding. 'But how?'

'The reporter is the only one who got out of that village alive,' answered Renny.

'But surely, if he'd been infected he would have died too,' said Iago. 'So how could it be him?'

Dropping his gaze to the ground, Renny shook his head.

'Oh – but it *was* him,' Gek stated.

He seemed to take pleasure in watching us trying to figure it out.

'We—' and here he swept his hand around to include Dr Faible, '—designed the virus... we developed the virus... we transmitted the virus to its host and *now* we've successfully tested the virus.' Gek was on a roll now – he obviously needed to boast of his achievements to someone. He pointed his finger at Iago. 'And do you know what? It works!'

'So this was all just a *test*?' Iago's face was red and he clenched his teeth so hard that his jawbone was visible through his skin.

'Yes. Of course it was a test. We had to test it to see if it worked.' He looked from one to the other of us, a dark gleam in his eye. 'Oh come on! You all look so horrified.'

'But hundreds of people died in this *test,*' I spat.

The words made my mouth feel dirty.

'Well,' answered Gek, 'we were never going to find any willing guinea pigs – were we?'

'So if the reporter was the host – why didn't he die?' I asked.

'Vaccination!' answered Iago.

'Good answer,' replied Gek, like a reluctant schoolteacher, encouraging a struggling student. 'But wrong, wrong, wrong! Anyone else?'

'If he wasn't vaccinated then he should have died,' mused Renny.

'And that's where the very clever Dr Faible comes in!'

Gek walked up to Faible, grabbing him by the shoulder, and dragged him forward roughly.

'You have the floor now, Doctor,' he said.

His invitation sounded more like a threat.

17

Faible cleared his throat nervously. Shuffling from foot to foot, he inhaled deeply, readying himself. He opened his mouth to begin, but then shut it again.

'FAIBLE!' yelled Gek, making the man leap visibly.

'Oh... um... where to begin.'

'Why didn't Evan Andrews die from the virus?' asked Renny quietly.

Faible looked at Renny.

'The virus is genetically engineered,' he answered simply.

'I've heard of that,' I said. 'It's where you change something, so it acts differently from the way it should.'

Faible nodded.

'What did you genetically engineer this virus to do?' asked Iago.

'To target certain groups...' the scientist answered, letting his shoulders slump forward.

'And Evan Andrews survived because he was *not* a member of this group?' Iago asked.

'Wait – wait,' said Renny. 'Viruses can be species specific – like Bluetongue, which only infects cattle or sheep. But I've never heard of one that targets members within a species.'

'Yes, that's right,' Iago added. 'We all have the same hearts and lungs and kidneys and brains. So why would a virus affect me and not you? I mean, if a virus attacks the heart of one human, surely it would do the same to the next and the next?'

'Yes it would,' answered Faible.

'So, why is this one different?' asked Renny.

'It's not the way the virus works that's different – it's how it targets its host.' Faible replied. 'Our virus targets a specific gene. Some people have it and others don't.'

'So you work on identifying *specific* genes?' Renny asked.

'He can't take all the credit!' Gek interrupted, clearly still feeling the need to boast about his part in all this. 'His work was important, but this wasn't his idea. He'd be still dabbling away in his lab, tracking down the gene for eye cancer, if I hadn't come along.'

Gek sat down at the end of the boardroom table nearest us and waved Faible to carry on.

'It's true – I was studying a very small area of chromosome 19,' Faible continued.

'Chromosome 19 is where the genes for eye colour are located,' Renny explained to Iago and me.

I nodded. I know that we get one set of chromosomes from our mother and one set from our father. And I know that chromosomes hold genes, which make us all different.

'I was trying to identify the gene that causes a very rare form of eye cancer,' said Faible. 'The cancer affects only people with light-coloured eyes.'

'Blue eyes – you mean?' Iago asked.

'Yes.'

'So why aren't brown-eyed people affected by this cancer?' I asked, a shiver running down my spine as I remembered the old lady's warning.

'Well – because the gene for light-coloured eyes is actually a genetic mutation. Originally, all humans had brown eyes, but a change to chromosome 19 occurred about six thousand years ago. So we know that all blue-eyed people have just *one* ancestor.'

'Just one ancestor!' I exclaimed.

'Yes,' replied Faible. 'We eventually found the gene for light coloured eyes on chromosome 19. So we were able to design a virus that attacks anyone who doesn't have that gene.'

'Hang on,' said Iago frowning. 'How did you go from cancer research to *this*?'

He glared at Gek, who just stared back at him.

Faible began to mumble. 'I needed money to fund my research.' He looked down, twiddling his fingers.

'Oh do we really have to go through the whole impoverished scientist on the verge of a major breakthrough story again?' sneered Gek. 'I gave him that money in return for a favour. All he had to do was combine his interests with mine!'

'And I presume that viruses are your main interest?' snapped Iago.

'At the moment – yes,' answered Gek.

Our discussion ended abruptly when one of the security guards strode up to Gek and whispered in his ear. Gek flashed a sickening grin, his eyes glinting.

'I'm afraid,' he exclaimed, placing his hands on the boardroom table, and pushing himself up energetically, 'I'll have to leave it there. If you are as clever as you think you are I'm sure you'll work it all out... eventually!'

Grabbing Faible by the shoulders, he pulled him to his feet.

'I'll be needing your services, Doctor. The test phase is over. We passed with flying colours. Now we can begin live operations.'

'By the way,' he said, stopping in the doorway, and turning back towards us. 'Don't bother planning an escape. You won't succeed. And even if you did, the police would never believe your story. Not after I talk to them!'

The door slammed shut behind Gek and Faible, and three of the security guards.

Apart from one guard, who was busy at a computer terminal near the door, we were left alone in the large room. Iago's stony face and steely eyes painted a pretty clear picture of what was going on in his mind.

'Why did they tell us all this?' I asked.

'That's just what I was wondering about,' said Iago. 'They wouldn't be telling us this if they were planning to let us go.'

'Or maybe – by the time they let us go, it won't matter,' said Renny.

'Any news from Cam, Rens?' I whispered, not wanting the guard to hear me. Maybe Cam would be able to send help.

'No,' whispered my brother in reply. 'Before they took my phone, I was able to track him. They should get to the hospital soon.'

'I suppose that no news is good news.' My voice cracked a little as I spoke.

When I looked over at my cousin, I could see that

his teeth were clenched again. This time a nerve in his jawbone twitched. He wouldn't be able to sit here for much longer. He would have to *do* something. At that moment, I couldn't imagine what that could be. I just hoped it wasn't going to be something foolish.

'Iago,' whispered Renny. 'Take a look...'

Iago, who was sitting further away from the laptop Gek had left on, had to lean over Renny. He squinted as he studied the screen. The audio was still muted so we couldn't hear what was going on. I was sitting too far away to make out what the writing on the bottom of the screen said.

'What does it say?' I asked.

'It says that the US President is fighting for his life!' Iago replied numbly.

I felt suddenly worried for the future of the world. The President was the only one pushing the climate change process forward. And, because of his mix of genes, many populations around the world felt he was one of them. His African ancestry meant he was committed to solar-energy production schemes, which could generate wealth for the people of that continent, and help reduce carbon emissions. The summers he spent with his grandmother in South America meant he not only spoke fluent Spanish and Portuguese, but also understood the history and needs of the people who lived there. He worked with all nations to try to preserve the world's natural resources. What would we do without him?

'There are also rumours that there have been five deaths among the world leaders, four men and one woman,' he continued. 'They haven't released names yet.'

'Do you *really* think Gek is responsible for this?' I asked. 'I mean – what if he's just claiming responsibility to frighten us more?'

'Tara,' replied Renny, 'have you forgotten what we saw in that room upstairs?'

I hadn't forgotten James, not for one minute. We didn't know what Gek planned to do, but we did know that he was serious – deadly serious.

18

A tiny tap on the door disrupted my train of thought. It was loud enough to attract the attention of the guard who'd been busy at one of the computers. He paused. He seemed unsure whether he'd heard anything. When the tapping sound came again, he stood up and walked to the door, placing his hand on the handle.

Opening it wide, he stepped back slightly. When no one entered the room, his eyebrows shot up. Then he scratched his head in confusion. He was clearly employed by Gek for his brawn, not his brains. Finally, he stepped into the doorway to check the corridor.

The dog was on top of him before he even saw it. The sudden shock, combined with the force of the animal, knocked him straight to the ground, his head colliding loudly with a desk on its way. He was out cold before he knew what happened.

I just stared at Renny and Iago. They looked every bit as surprised as I was.

'Hi guys!' came the soft voice of my cousin.

'Aretha!' said Iago, beaming. 'How did you get here?'

'The same way you did,' she answered. 'I'm not just a pretty face, you know.'

'Aretha – I love you!' I said. 'Now get us out of these.'

I looked down, indicating my tied wrists.

She smiled at me, then frowned straight away. 'I saw Cam running into the wood with Charlie in his arms. I didn't dare call out to him, in case someone heard me. What happened?'

'We'll tell you later,' said Iago. 'Right now – we need to get out of here.'

'OK,' she said and ran to help her brother.

She sliced through his restraints with the small but sharp knife on her camping multi-tool. Iago darted from his chair and set to work on Renny's bindings while Aretha crouched beside me, her eyes shining. She was enjoying being the rescuer.

Flinging off the ropes, I massaged my reddened wrists and rushed to Iago.

'The other guards can't have gone far,' I whispered.

'I know,' he answered, checking the guard's pulse. 'He's OK – I think he's just stunned. We need to get out of here.'

Renny retrieved his precious phone from the boardroom table, along with Iago's. Then, grabbing our rucksacks from the corner, we made our way cautiously towards the open door. We had no idea whether the other guard was on his way back, so we had to escape. We wouldn't get another chance.

We all lined up flush with the door, Iago closest. On a count of three, he peeped around the doorframe. He withdrew his head straight away. His raised finger on his lips told us that there was someone in the corridor. We didn't know how close this person might be. I held my breath. The dog cocked his ears, growling softly. He had better hearing than we did, so I paid attention.

Time dragged as we stood there. My heart pounded due to lack of oxygen as my body cried out for more. I had held my breath for so long now that my lungs were desperate. But, I knew if I opened my mouth, my lungs would suck in air, in a loud gasping rasp. I was doomed if I did and dead if I didn't.

Instinct took over: doom was better than death. Opening my mouth like a feeding fish, my lungs greedily grasped every molecule of oxygen they could. The noise that resulted echoed in the still air.

Three angry heads snapped towards me. I could see how disappointed Aretha was. She had overcome her fear *and* found a way to rescue us, and now I was ruining her moment. I felt dirtier than a kitty litter tray. Even the dog gave me a look.

We all stood in absolute silence for a few seconds, listening.

To my surprise, the dog then cocked his ears and walked forward confidently, his tail wagging. He gave me a smug glance as he passed. Oh great! Now even this dog felt superior to me.

Four sets of eyes followed the dog as he approached the doorframe, still relaxed and cool. Iago frowned as the dog sauntered past him. Whoever Iago had seen in the corridor must have gone. The dog was trying to tell us that.

Peeling myself off the wall, I tiptoed towards the dog. Iago was still looking a bit annoyed at my outburst. I was sorry for what I'd done, but we didn't have time for this. I needed to make up for my mistake. With my heart pounding, I rushed through the door.

For a split second, I thought I'd been wrong to trust the dog. A muffled sound echoed along the mezzanine, stopping me in my tracks. It was a rhythmic noise and it sounded a bit like marching feet. I froze mid-step, waiting for my grey matter to process the information.

After a couple of seconds, I realised that the sound was too regular to be human – it must have been mechanical. Probably air-conditioning or heating. The dog darting past me made me jump, and the flight instinct kicked in. I became a lemming. I would have followed the dog over the edge of a cliff without a second's hesitation.

I wasn't the only lemming in the group. As I ran, I heard the footsteps of the others behind me.

The green light above a door near the lift was my only focus at that moment. I hoped it was what I thought it was. The writing beneath the light became clearer as we pounded towards it. Though the image juddered every time my foot landed, I could start to make out the words 'Emergency Exit'. I hoped it wasn't alarmed, since we didn't really want them to know we'd escaped.

Iago overtook me before I'd reached the exit. He flung himself at the door, pushing the bar down to release the lock.

19

No alarm sounded.

We raced down the stairs. There were two doors at the bottom, one probably leading into the reception area and one marked 'Emergency Exit' to the right of it. Iago opened it and we rushed out into the night. The door was set into the side of the building and opened onto the clearing facing the wood we'd come through earlier.

We were almost halfway towards the shelter of the trees when a blaze of blinding white light surrounded us. Raising our arms to protect our eyes, we stood stunned, like rabbits in a car's headlights, our sprint halted for just a split second. Then instinct took over. In sheer blind panic, we all hurtled desperately towards the protection of those trees.

A loud, static hiss echoed in the still night. It was the sound of a microphone being switched on. Then through the pounding of my pulse in my eardrum, came the voice of the horrible Gek.

'Run... run... children. I'm a little busy right now but I *will* find you.'

'Keep going,' shouted Iago, without breaking his stride.

His voice was almost drowned out by the hum of static, but his tone gave me confidence – he seemed to have a plan.

Reaching the trees first, Iago stopped, signalling to the rest of us to follow him in. Didn't he know we were going flat out? He was forgetting that we weren't all like Charlie – we couldn't all run like the wind. The light was behind us now, no longer blinding us. Instead, we were highlighted against the dark wood.

I got to Iago first, with Renny and Aretha just behind me, holding hands. Roughly, he dragged us one by one through the screen of outermost trees. Stumbling over a tree root, I landed heavily on the ground. Thankfully, the forest floor was soft from years of fallen leaves.

After the muted thud of my landing, I lay there gratefully, drawing the earthy scent in through my nose, feeling safe, just for a second.

Picking myself up, I joined the others.

'Maybe they won't follow us,' I whispered.

'Gek didn't seem to be in a hurry, but that doesn't mean he won't send someone soon. Let's keep moving,' answered Iago.

We made our way carefully over fallen branches and patches of brambles. We couldn't run – there wasn't enough light, but then we didn't really need to. There didn't seem to be anyone following us, at least for the moment.

Iago took out his phone. 'Hello? Police please,' he said quietly.

We all listened while Iago explained what we'd just witnessed to the person on the other end of the line.

When he hung up he said, 'They didn't seem to take

me very seriously. Gek must have called them, like he said he would.'

'Do you mean they won't come and help us?' I asked.

'They didn't say that, but I got the impression that we weren't their top priority.'

As we made our way deeper and deeper into the wood, the facility's bright security lights began to fade. The darkness was enveloping, like a thick blanket.

There is something very appealing about woods. Maybe it comes from our ancestors. Maybe, like deer, they knew that they could find shelter from predators, their footsteps muffled by the soft earth and their movements camouflaged the light playing through the leaves.

I was still very frightened, but more than that, I felt aware – like an animal. My senses compensated for the darkness. I could hear sounds I hadn't noticed before: the tiny squeak of bats. I remembered that adults couldn't hear that.

Next, I heard a rustling in the undergrowth – probably a small animal out searching for a midnight feast. The smell of wild garlic floated past me, bringing back memories of running through a pine forest on holiday in France.

'Pssst,' signalled Renny.

We all crouched down around him, studying his phone's small screen. Cam's drawn face appeared, and he whispered, 'Renny? Renny? Can you see me? I can't see you. Are you still inside that place?'

'We're all here,' whispered Iago, taking Renny's phone. 'We've escaped. Let me know where you are and we'll come and meet you.'

'Iago, it's no good,' replied Cam, his voice cracking.

'What's no good, Cam?'

'It's Charlie. She's getting worse. I don't know what to do. We're at the hospital.'

'How did you get there?' I asked.

'Once we were out of the wood, I called the taxi that dropped Charlie off earlier on. I told him she'd eaten a wild mushroom. He took me straight to the hospital. I told the doctors the truth though, that she'd been scratched by an infected animal. They're doing all they can—'

'What do you mean, "all they can"?' whispered Iago. 'Why isn't she getting better, then?'

'Because they don't have an antidote,' Cam replied.

'I suppose they've given her standard antivirals,' said Renny.

'What do *they* do?' Iago asked.

'Antivirals help the body to fight a virus and usually weaken the symptoms, but they can't cure it,' Renny explained. 'Only the body itself can do that.'

'They've given her normal antivirals,' Cam confirmed. 'But the doctors here can't even identify the virus. They just said that we'd have to wait and hope.'

'No!' said Renny. 'Haven't these people heard of nanoviricides?'

'What are nanoviricides?' I asked.

'Nanoviricides are the newest weapon in our arsenal against disease. They're engineered to attach to a specific virus,' he answered.

'Who'd have nanoviricides?' I asked.

'The same person who develops viruses!' said Renny.

'Of course – Dr Faible,' exclaimed Iago.

'Someone needs to go back in there!' I whispered.

'I'll go,' volunteered Renny.

'No!' answered Iago sharply.

'Why not?' Renny asked.

'You're more valuable out here.'

Iago held the phone up to his face.

'Cam – I *will* find this nanoviricide and I *will* get it to you. Just – please – keep her alive...'

His voice trailed off at the end and he turned away from us. When he turned back towards us, his face was set but his eyes were glistening.

'Tara – you're with me,' he said. 'Renny – if I find this nanoviricide, I'm going to need to get to Charlie fast. Talk to Cam. Call on your Geeksquad. Do whatever you can. My only goal now is to keep Charlie alive.'

'But what about James?' I asked.

'We'll find a way, Tara.'

Then he turned to his sister. 'Aretha, you look after Renny and keep the dog close by. We might need rescuing again.'

He leaned over and kissed her on the top of the head.

'Come on Tara,' he said.

I turned to wave to the others as Iago ran off, back the way we'd come. Then, stuffing my phone in my jeans pocket, I followed. But I couldn't find him. In his haste to help Charlie, he'd moved away too quickly.

'Iago... Iago?' I called softly as I made my way through the brush.

Suddenly a hand gently covered my mouth. I felt myself being dragged backwards behind a tree. 'Sh,' whispered Iago in my ear. 'It's me!'

A twig snapped somewhere to my right. Of course,

it could have been an animal, but something told me it wasn't. It was big and it was moving very stealthily. It was stalking something or someone. The hiss and crackle of a two-way radio confirmed what Iago had suspected – Gek's men were looking for us.

Leaning close to my ear so that he barely needed to whisper Iago said, 'We need to draw them away from Renny and Aretha, but we can *not* afford to get caught!'

He was right – Renny needed to stay outside to coordinate things. With his network of geek friends – the Geeksquad – around the globe, he could make things happen. We couldn't allow him to be captured. But if we were to stand any chance of saving Charlie, Iago needed to be able to get to her, so he couldn't take any chances either! That left only one option as far as I was concerned.

If anyone was going to be caught – it had to be me.

20

Suddenly I became afraid for my own life. Just because they hadn't hurt us up until now, it didn't mean that they wouldn't. Then the image of Charlie's unconscious body in Cam's arms came back to me, and I knew what I had to do.

I bolted out of Iago's grip and ran towards the sounds we'd just heard. He didn't call out to me; maybe he'd come to the same conclusion that I had – I was the obvious bait. He'd never have suggested that I give myself up so that he could escape, but in that moment, I knew that he had to let me go. Charlie's life depended on it!

Blindly, I stumbled forward over roots and fallen branches. I had no plan, only to attract the guards' attention and try to draw them away from Iago.

As I staggered past a line of trees, a hand shot out, grabbing me roughly. The brawny guard who'd been knocked out by the dog was my captor. He growled angrily at me as his massive hands grabbed my wrists. But I didn't care now how roughly he dragged me. I stood still while he tied my hands together and I didn't flinch when Gek's slimy voice came over the two-way radio. He thought he'd captured me, but like a secret agent, I'd allowed myself to fall into their hands. I now had a critical role to play in order for the mission to succeed.

The short trip back to the facility passed in a blur of trees and heavy footsteps. Gek was waiting by the main door. With the eerie blue glow from inside the facility outlining his frame, he looked harder, like he was made of some kind of mineral. Shafts of light shone like strobes, silhouetting him. His silver hair sparkled, making him look demonic. He grinned at me as I passed, but didn't speak. I lifted my chin in defiance.

Saying nothing, I allowed myself to be dragged by the guard through the entrance, past the smart reception area and along the corridor.

Gek didn't utter a word as we waited for the lift, or on the short journey to the first floor. When we left the lift, he walked ahead of me, in silence. Finally, as we arrived back at his boardroom-cum-hub, he turned to me.

'By the way – if you think your friends can raise the alarm and send in the cavalry, you'll be disappointed. We've already called the police and told them that some kids were here causing mischief. I think your friends will find that they're not taken very seriously. Besides my men are out searching for them – it's only a matter of time before you're all reunited.'

My heart sank. Iago had been right.

Then, with no warning, Gek grabbed my arm, dragging me towards his office. Once inside he locked the door and flicked a switch. The glass walls of his office frosted over. I could still see the shapes of people and furniture outside, but they were blurred. I looked at

Gek, who now settled himself behind his desk.

'Sit down, young lady,' he growled, opening his laptop.

I was about to look around for a chair when the screen filled with a map of the world. Gek was completely absorbed in his work, so I decided to stay put.

Those maps are always a bit weird to look at. It's almost impossible to fit the three dimensional globe onto a two dimensional map and still get the shape, size, and location of each bit of land right.

The geography of Africa is not my strongest subject, but today it didn't need to be. I knew that the area highlighted was Somalia. I knew he'd been responsible for the terrible outbreak there, and thinking about the victims made my stomach churn painfully.

Somalia was highlighted in orange and I could make out a legend at the bottom of the screen. The legend showed colours, each one corresponding to a status. Next to the blue strip the words 'No current operations' appeared. Underneath that was a green strip with the words 'Possible future operation' next to it. Third in the legend was orange with the words 'Completed test operation' and finally the red strip with the words 'Current operation in progress' next to it.

My eyes darted around the flattened earth searching for the red. It didn't take long to locate it. Unfortunately, I couldn't quite work out where the highlighted region was. It was definitely east of Africa, but not as far over as India, so I guessed that it was somewhere in the Middle East. I thought I could see a capital letter D, but then he clicked the file closed.

I didn't know what Gek was planning, but now that

I had an idea where he was going to do it, I had to tell
the others.

21

Gek stood up suddenly. He walked slowly towards me and leaned so close that I could smell his expensive aftershave.

'I thought I told you to sit down,' he hissed.

I backed into a chair near the desk, and slumped into it.

'Don't go anywhere,' he whispered through his gleaming teeth.

The hairs on the back of my neck stood up, one by one. Even his whisper carried the threat of danger.

Not long after he'd left the room, the brawny guard came through the door. He was chewing – he'd probably just been stuffing his face with steak and eggs, followed by a protein shake.

Without a word, he pulled my rucksack off my back. Then he took out some ropes and tied my hands together. Then smirking, he squatted down and tied each of my legs to the chair.

'Boss had a change of heart,' he muttered, standing up. 'He thinks you're trouble!'

He sneered at me again, then left the room. Great! Now I was tied up and I'd lost my rucksack again. But I was alone – for the moment. I *had* to do something. I wouldn't get another chance. I could get my phone out of my pocket, but operating it would be tricky.

After much struggling, I managed to get it out. I could see that I'd missed a call from Iago and there was a message waiting. I really wanted to know where he was and what he was up to, so I hit voicemail.

I could make out some background noises the phone's mike had picked up, what sounded like a squeaking door, followed by echoing footsteps.

'Tara – I'm in. Thanks for that, back there in the wood. I know it wasn't easy to do. I don't know if I'd have been brave enough to give myself up, but I know you did this for Charlie. Listen... I've no idea how this is going to work but I'm keeping my phone on vibrate. I think we're going to need to communicate at some point. Call me as soon as you're able to. If I haven't heard from you in the next thirty minutes, I'll try again... Hope you're OK...'

A small lump formed in my throat and I tried to swallow it away. I wanted to let him know that I was all right, but I also desperately wanted to know how he was doing. I wasn't going to even think of escape until I knew he had found the nanoviricide, and was on his way to Charlie. I laughed at myself then: like I'd be *able* to escape anyway!

Shrugging off negative thoughts, I dialled Iago.

'Tara, where are you?'

'In Gek's office.'

'You OK?'

'Yes. Have you found the nanoviricides?'

'Not yet, Tara, but I'll let you know as soon as I do.'

'Iago, Gek has more vile plans. He's planning another

virus strike somewhere in the Middle East. I don't know what I should do?'

'Tell Renny,' he said. 'Tara – I have to go now.'

The line went dead. I didn't want Renny or Aretha to know about my self-sacrifice. They needed to stay where they were – on the outside. I didn't know if I could keep the fear out of my voice, so I opened my gmail and sent Renny an IM about Gek's plans in the Middle East. Of course, Renny was logged in to his account, under his geek alias: Geekboss. His reply popped up in the chat bubble instantly.

Geekboss *are you and iago ok? how do you know about gek's plans? where in middle east – it's a big place.*

Tara *no idea where. can you do some searching?*

He didn't reply straight away, so I guessed that he was doing some investigating. My phone vibrated in my hand. It was Iago calling.

'Tara,' he began. 'I found Faible. We're in his office. At the moment, he's not that much help – he just keeps saying how sorry he is; that he never meant to hurt anyone. With ambition blinding him, he didn't even ask what the research was for. Funny how people can forget the important questions when it suits them.'

'What a horrible, selfish man,' I replied.

'He said that he tried to get away, but now Gek's holding him prisoner here. He says he wants to help me. I think he wants to make amends for what he's done.'

'He's still horrible,' I answered.

'I know. I just can't get my head around this. What they did here was unbelievable. I mean, not just hard to imagine but actually *not* believable. It's like some horror story. They ran tests on animals first, and when those were successful they abducted a child and took his blood.'

'I can't believe it either,' I answered.

Iago was silent for a moment.

'Faible just told me,' he continued, 'that Gek asked him to manufacture viruses that would attach themselves to the blue-eyed gene. The virus that Charlie contracted from the dog was an early experimental one. The lab-rats and dogs were meant to be destroyed, but they hadn't got round to it yet.'

'What were they up to?' I asked.

'Faible says it was a simple virus. All they did was modify it so that it would attach itself to the blue-eyed gene. Just a trial to see if they could deliver a virus in this way. Once they discovered it worked, they just reversed their science. They developed viruses that *wouldn't* attach to the blue-eyed gene.'

'So that's good then, isn't it, Iago?' I said. 'Charlie's virus is just a simple one.'

He didn't reply straight away.

'Tara... the survival rate of the lab animals was only twenty per cent.'

Beads of sweat broke out on my forehead as I tried to get to grips with what he was telling me: Charlie had only a twenty per cent chance of living!

'Anyway,' he continued, 'Faible does have a nanoviricide, a kind of antidote that might save Charlie. Gek knows about it – they tested it on one of the dogs.'

Iago's voice came back quiet and even.

'For the attack on the G20, Gek chose a variety of viruses. Some blue-eyed children in a choir were used to transmit them. Like Evan Andrews, they were just carriers. The viruses didn't harm them because the blue-eyed gene makes them immune.'

He paused and when he spoke again, I could hear the emotion in his voice.

'But Tara – the viruses were engineered specifically for the G20 delegates. Gek managed to get hold of some of their DNA. His men have been working for months, infiltrating the delegates' security teams. They managed to get some samples of their hair. And from those they were able to isolate unique genes. To those people, the viruses the children carried are lethal.'

My head was starting to hurt. This just kept getting worse.

'Faible developed other nanoviricides that Gek doesn't know about. Nanoviricides that might save the President and the other delegates. But he says that, even with the nanoviricides, it would take an incredibly strong individual to fight the viruses.'

I could hear Iago's footsteps as he paced up and down. Then my cousin took a couple of deep breaths.

'Tara,' said Iago softly, 'I need to contact Renny now. Faible is willing to get me the nanoviricide I need to save Charlie, but we need to get to her fast. I'm sorry, but I can't come to get you. I can't risk getting caught. If I did – Charlie would die. I hope you understand. But, as soon as I get out – I'll call the police again.'

Of course I understood – I would have done anything to save Charlie or any of the others. But suddenly I was afraid. I didn't want to be stuck here on my own. I needed help. As soon as I knew that Iago was out of the building, I'd ask Renny to help me – my brother was always good in a tight spot. And I'd never been in a spot tighter than this!

22

I dialled Renny. I just heard his 'Hello', when the door flew open. I had to scramble to get my phone into my pocket. Gek was back.

Then I had an idea. Since he was here, I'd try to find out a bit more about what was going on before I called Renny back. I was still tied to the chair, but I wasn't gagged. I could get more information, if I used the right tactics. I had to *be* that spy.

'So,' I began, trying to sound interested, 'why did you choose Evan Andrews?'

Gek just looked at me. His creepy stare made me feel physically sick. For a second, I thought my plan was foiled because he just stood there, staring.

Then, shrugging his shoulders, he answered, 'Evan Andrews was the perfect target – a really famous journalist who can go anywhere. He can enter war zones, slip across borders, and get into military bases with just a flash of his credentials. What better host could I ask for?'

He pulled up a chair and swivelled it around, sitting on it backwards, his arms resting on the back, his over-tanned face only inches from mine.

'All I had to do was ask if he wanted to do a story

about me and my fortune.'

Gek was bragging now. He was enjoying telling his evil story. I began to fear for my own future. Why was he so willing to tell me everything? I tried to keep my reactions in check as he continued.

'It was an informal first meeting at my home – just dinner and a chat. He was very charming, you know, and he does have the most remarkable violet-blue eyes.'

He bared his teeth and I cringed. He made my skin creep. Swallowing hard, I carried on.

'But how did you get the virus into him?'

'Hah!' he laughed. 'We used the oldest trick in the book – we dissolved our concoction in a drink. Still the most reliable way of making sure you target the right person.'

I was finding it hard to keep the feelings of disgust from showing on my face. But Gek was opening up so I had to keep going.

Think, Tara – what other information might be useful to Renny? My brain ticked through some questions before it found the right one.

'Why did the virus only kill those people in Somalia and not everyone else he came in contact with?'

'Ah – that's where the clever Doctor Faible's research came into its own,' he sneered. 'You see – his genotyping program traced the blue-eyed gene quite easily. The only problem was that we didn't want to attack every brown-eyed person in the world. That would have been a bit stupid, wouldn't it?'

He leaned closer to me so I could see his hard eyes more clearly. They were brown! I just nodded in agreement. He was so close now, my legs began to tremble.

'We needed to identify other genes as well,' he carried on. 'So we decided to look at other populations – isolated populations.'

'What — like people on an island or something?' I gulped.

'Something like that. The fact is, the more isolated a tribe is – the fewer ancestors it has, so the more similar the genes are. All we had to do was identify a particular gene. Then we could look for it in a larger population. Once we found it, we had our target. We just had to modify the virus so that it only worked so long as the person had brown eyes plus whatever other gene we chose.'

Again, he sneered triumphantly, making me clench my teeth.

'So your virus just lay dormant in Evan Andrews' blood?' I asked.

I was finding it hard to keep the disgust out of my voice. Gek stood up suddenly, leering down at me.

'Yes, it was unable to attach itself, since he didn't have the right docking port. But, as soon as he came in contact with the target population, it poured out of him. It was incredibly efficient. No one lasted longer than thirty minutes. Imagine how devastated he's going to be when he finds out it was all his fault!'

He walked towards the door, then turned back, his eyes flashing.

'Oh, and – just wait until he finds out what I've got lined up for him next...'

With that, he walked out.

I just sat there staring, my face frozen in horror. What

did he mean? Had he infected Evan Andrews with more than one virus?

I needed to get word to Renny. We had to find Evan Andrews. And by hook or by crook, we *had* to find a way of getting him back here. Someone was going to have to go through his blood with a fine toothcomb before letting him travel around the globe again!

I fumbled my phone out again and logged on to my gmail account. I tried to get the gist of what Gek had told me in as short a message as possible. As I waited for a reply, my phone vibrated again. It was Iago.

'Tara – I'm out. Sorry to leave you in there, but Cam's arranged for the taxi to come back and pick us up. Faible is with me. We have the nanoviricides we need to help Charlie and the others. I only hope that it's not too late.' Iago gulped, then carried on. 'As soon as we give Charlie the nanoviricide, we'll try to get to the G20 victims.'

He paused, then asked, 'How are you doing?'

'Um – I'm OK,' I answered.

'Listen,' he continued, 'Faible says that the virus they concocted for the President was so strong it will be more difficult to treat him. I won't give up though. We have to try. The President is a good man. He's trying to make the world a better place to live in. I'm afraid that if he dies like this, all the good he's trying to do will just fade away.'

Tears rolled down my cheeks as I listened to my cousin. Surprised, I raised my tied hands to brush them away. I understood what he was saying. There was so much war, so much hatred, and so much destruction in the world. This was the first president ever to have a truly global perspective. I couldn't begin to imagine a world without him.

I raised my tied up hands, clasping them tightly together, whispering, *'Please – just let him live.'*

'What?' came Iago's voice.

'Nothing,' I replied.

'Tara? I thought you said something? Listen, be strong.'

I sniffed.

'I'm proud of you,' he said, before ending the call.

I swallowed down a lump in my throat as Renny's IM came through.

Geekboss *geeksquad working on locating andrews. screen-scraping every airline's website as we speak. will take time. don't know what we do when we find him. no contact with dad but checked around with ones who know – quarantine the only solution. snag is – needs to be policed by people immune to bug. since we don't know who target population is, don't know who is immune. gotta go...*

I needed to get more information for Renny. I had to find out who the next target was, or at least where they lived. If we knew which genetic marker Gek was targeting, then we could warn the authorities. They could try to make sure that the people who detained Evan Andrews didn't carry that gene.

Gek had left his laptop on the desk, but he'd closed the file I needed. What could I do? Then I realised that I'd had a fairly good look at the map. All I needed to do was find a map of the region online and look it up.

I was tied to the chair, but I could shuffle it forward. It took a while, but I made it to the desk eventually.

Using the internet with your hands tied is difficult, but I managed to open the browser.

I searched Google for maps of the Middle East. Several came up, so I clicked on one and found Egypt easily enough. The Red Sea lay between Egypt and Saudi Arabia. I scrolled across it. I knew that Saudi Arabia was a big place, but I couldn't remember where the capital city was. Was it on the northern coast? But I was sure that I'd seen the letter D on Gek's screen... Did the capital of Saudi Arabia begin with a D?

'*Riyadh!*' I remembered.

I found it on the map. No – that was in the wrong place. His target had been on the coast, and began with the letter D. I had to look harder.

I searched the rest of Saudi Arabia but couldn't find a match. Then I looked around Oman. No luck there either. There was Doha – the capital of Qatar. But for some reason that didn't sound right to me. I closed my eyes, trying to force the image back into my mind.

I magnified the region of the map I thought I'd seen. Then I realised my mistake – I'd been looking for a capital city. But this place wasn't the capital. Still, it was a very well known place.

I'd found the location for Gek's next attack.

23

Fumbling for my phone, I called Renny.

'It's Dubai,' I said.

I hoped Renny understood, because I could hear footsteps outside the office. They were getting closer, so I hung up. In a panic, I shut down the Google search page. My legs worked furiously to shuffle the chair back into the right place, while my hands worked against each other as I tried to get the phone back in my pocket.

Gek walked back into the room, and I stopped mid shuffle. I hoped he hadn't seen me moving.

As it turned out, he barely glanced at me, although even this small look was shrivelling. On reflex, my gaze dropped to the floor. He checked a few files on his laptop before snapping it shut. Picking it up, he walked towards the door.

Again, he looked at me. His face was a mask but his eyes narrowed. His jaw line set and his mouth curled up on one side. I'd never seen anyone smile so menacingly before. A sudden chill ran down my spine.

'Rest assured one of my guards will be just outside, so don't do anything foolish.'

Then he headed out through the door.

There was something evil in that last look of his.

I got the feeling that he had a sinister plan, and that I shouldn't hang around here to find out what it was.

I could see Gek's back grow smaller and smaller through the frosted glass and finally I heard the outer door shut. He was gone, but he'd said one of his guards would be outside. Did he mean outside the door of his office or the door of the office-cum-boardroom? I decided to take a look. I, and my chair, shuffled awkwardly over to where I'd seen Gek press a button to frost the glass. I hesitated just a second. What if one of them was right outside? I decided to take a chance anyway. I hit the button. That last encounter with Gek had frightened me more than one of his guards ever could.

I couldn't see anyone moving around, but some of the screens were still on. The biggest one on the wall at the back of the boardroom showed images of people being stretchered out of a flying ambulance. I was too far away to make out any of the headline text running along the bottom, but across the top of the image, I could read the location on the top. It said Addenbrooke's Hospital, Cambridge.

This could have been any group of seriously ill or injured people, but they were encased in protective bubbles and everyone else was wearing a Hazmat suit. They had to be the surviving G20 delegates. Was the President among them?

My phone vibrated in my pocket. Since I was alone again, I could answer it. I fished it out as quickly as my nervous hands allowed me.

'Hello?' I whispered softly. 'What's going on?'

'Thanks for the Dubai tip. My guys—'

'Renny, are your *guys* still the GST or are there some

other anti-heroes working for you these days? Is there a Renny's army of nerds, sitting at their computers eating jellybeans and waiting for their chance to answer your call – to become *Geekman*?'

'Hey, listen – Geekman has saved the universe more times than Superman ever did. Remember CERN? These guys are real, and without their help not only you, but everyone on this planet – in fact the *actual* planet would be history right now...'

'Sorry, Renny, I'm a bit uptight. I know your friends are valuable.'

Anyway,' he interrupted. 'The *guys* tracked Andrews to a US air-force base at Incirlik in Turkey. Since there isn't exactly a passenger manifest for military flights, we had kind of hit a brick wall. But... since you told me that Dubai was the potential target, I've found out that there's a flight currently heading for Dubai from Incirlik. Now, I can't be sure that Evan Andrews is on that plane, but it did leave just after he arrived and...'

'And *what*, Renny?'

'I did some checking. Get this! Evan Andrews is booked into a luxury suite at the Golden Strands resort and casino – *the* most exclusive and expensive resort in the world.'

'But – how can Evan Andrews afford a suite at a place like that?' I asked. 'I mean, Dubai is already one of the most exclusive places in the world, so can you imagine how much a suite like that costs?'

'That's the interesting part. He didn't pay for it!'

'Who did then?'

'It was paid for by a company called Parasol Private Equities Inc. And guess who the sole owner of that company is?'

'Peter Gek?'

'You got it!'

'This is all part of his plan then. But Renny – Andrews has been infected with several viruses.'

'Or several versions of the same virus,' he said. 'Just targeted at different populations.'

'He's like a ticking bomb. If he enters the right genetic zone, he goes off. You have to find a way to stop that plane.'

'Oh, that should be a piece of cake,' sighed Renny. 'I'll just call up the US military base and tell them that they need to stop Flight 871 from landing in Dubai. "Sure!" they'll say. "No problem. We always pay attention to teenagers who call us with ridiculous stories about genetically engineered viruses and journalists."'

'Renny – I didn't say it would be easy, but you have to try.'

I'm sure Iago would have made Renny feel more hopeful. But Iago had other things on his mind right now. There was no way on earth that I was going to distract him. He had to save Charlie.

'Call me when you know more, Rens,' I said softly.

'Will do,' he answered.

I was worried – Renny wasn't too confident about stopping Evan Andrews. But I had some problems of my own to deal with. I was still very much a prisoner. I needed to find a way out of this place, not just for myself but for James as well.

Before I had a chance to even think of any kind of plan, my phone rang again. It was Iago. I panicked as I answered. Why was he calling me? He wouldn't need to call me unless there was a problem. What had gone wrong?

24

'Tara?'

'Iago – how is Charlie?'

'I don't know.' His voice was quiet, but his tone said everything. 'I've given the nanoviricides to the doctors. They're treating Charlie right now. There's nothing more I can do to help her. But we might be able to help the President.'

'Where are you?' I asked.

'I'm in a taxi, heading for Cambridge. The G20 victims were taken to Addenbrooke's Hospital. They have the best infectious diseases unit in the country.'

'Oh yes – I saw it on TV. Is the President among them?'

'Yes. He's still alive, Tara, but the reports aren't good.'

'You can't always believe the media,' I said, trying to be positive.

'The reports are coming from the hospital. This time it's not the media trying to make the news more sensational than it really is. Listen, Tara, I need some help.'

'So why are you calling me? I'm stuck in here, waiting for help myself. Why don't you ask Renny?

He's usually much more useful than I am.'

'No, this time you're the only one who can help me.'

'But, how can *I* help?'

'I need you to find something.'

'Find what?' I asked. There was something wrong, and it must be serious because he knew I was trapped here.

'We need some of Faible's notes.'

'*Why*?' I asked.

'Um... because he doesn't know the exact nanoviricide to give the President,' said Iago. 'We need to give him the right one – the one that attaches to his gene – otherwise it just won't work.'

I tried to remember what Gek had said. The children of the choir had somehow been given different viruses. One of them must have been carrying the viral-bomb meant for the President.

'And he didn't think of this *before* you left?'

'He says he forgot. And I feel stupid for not making sure we had everything.'

'It must have been chaos trying to get out of there and get to Charlie in time,' I said.

'Yes – I just grabbed what he told me to. I wasn't thinking straight – saving Charlie was my only focus. I'm ashamed to say that saving the President's life wasn't my top priority. But now I'm prepared to do anything I can to save him.'

I understood what he meant. 'OK, Iago, I'll do whatever it takes. Just let me know what you need.'

'You need to get to Faible's office. It's next to the room that James is in. Do you remember how to get there?'

'I think so,' I said.

There's a file in a drawer. Just get there and then call me. We're getting close to Cambridge now. I hope we can get to the President. But I'm worried about the timing. I'll have to take on the combined security services of the world's major countries. They're not going to let me just walk into that hospital, no matter what I can promise them. Even if the President were on the brink of death, there's no way one of his aides would take a chance on injecting him with something that *might* save his life. What if it killed him instantly? They would forever be known as the person who killed the President.'

'You'll do it Iago – I know you will.' I answered, trying to sound positive.

'Listen Tara – I know it's not going to be easy for you either, but please do your best. Please get to Faible's office. I'll ask the others to help you as much as they can. Bye.'

Then he was gone and I felt alone. All my bravado when talking to Iago had gone. My palms were cold and clammy and my stomach felt strange.

Normally I am the kind of person who likes to stop and think. I like to go through a situation in my mind before I act. I'm not impulsive. But, now I realised that there were times when you just had to act. You couldn't plan situations like this. This 'mission' was constantly changing. I smiled – I was starting to think like a real spook now.

I put my phone back in my pocket. I had to get these ropes off. I looked around the room, desperately searching for something I could use to cut the ropes. But there was nothing. Frustrated, I tried to loosen the ropes on my hands. But they were still too tight. It was useless.

Then I tried moving my legs. I realised that all my shuffling around with the chair had loosened the leg restraints a little. I bent over and awkwardly, because my hands were still tied together, undid my right shoe. It is the first time that being really small has been useful. Not only am I very short but I'm also quite thin. First, I managed to pull my skinny ankle through the rope and, after a lot of struggling and some painful tugging, my tiny foot came free. I repeated the process with my left foot. This took a bit longer and was a lot more painful. But finally, my left foot was also free of its restraints. I looked down at my sore feet. Large red welts appeared and the skin was burning, but I didn't care. I could get out of here. I put my shoes back on as fast as I could. My hands were still tied, but that didn't matter for now – I'd keep wriggling them and dislocate a wrist if I had to.

I stood up and walked to the door. It opened noiselessly, so I stepped through it. I stopped and checked to my left, then my right, before leaving the relative safety of the doorway. Tiptoeing across the boardroom, my heart raced, making me breathe heavier. I made it to the boardroom doorway and had to stop to catch my breath. The free-flowing adrenaline was making me sweat. My legs were shaking.

Before I lost my confidence, I grabbed the door handle. It wasn't locked!

I pulled the door towards me, peeking around the doorpost. There didn't seem to be anyone there. Maybe they'd abandoned their post. Or Gek had sent them somewhere else. Either way, I had an opportunity to escape.

Still, a nagging feeling clawed at my back as I raced across the mezzanine towards the lift. When I reached it, I decided that it wasn't a very good idea to take it. What if it opened and I was met by a security guard? Or – worse still – Gek!

I opened the doorway to the emergency stairwell we'd used earlier and ran down quietly. Once I got to the ground-floor door that led to reception, I pushed it open, just a tiny bit. I could only see a slice of the reception area, but all the lights were out and the desk was unoccupied. Something didn't feel right. Why was there nobody about? Did they all clock off early? Had they all been called away to deal with something?

I bolted through the door and towards the corridor where the torture room and James were. As I ran, I strained against the ropes on my wrists. They were loosening a little. I could pull my right hand down slightly. But still not enough to free it.

I headed down the corridor towards the end. Problem was there were quite a few doors down there. I'd only been here once and I'd been fairly distracted at the time. I couldn't remember exactly which door led to the lab-rats prison, or the room James was in. And none of the doors was marked. I had no choice but to try some of them.

I didn't try the first door – I knew it wasn't that one. I'd have remembered if it had been. So I opted to start at the second one. I needed to think like a secret agent again. I was potentially walking into a dangerous situation. There was no knowing who or what lay beyond any of these doors.

I turned the handle slowly. There was a tiny ping as the mechanism released. I stopped. It had been a very quiet sound but in the silence of the corridor, it had seemed loud. I waited, my heart thumping, my leg muscles tense, ready to bolt.

There didn't seem to be any response from inside the room. But I had to stay alert, all the same. The first thing I did when I entered the room was to scan left and right for any guards. The second thing I did was to check for exits – always best to have more than one way out of a room, even if it's only a window. Only after this did I start checking whether this could be Faible's office.

The first room I went in wasn't the right one, so I tried the next. It was just another standard office, with a few bits of scientific equipment lying around. There was a microscope on the desk, and some round flat glass dishes, with lids on. I was beginning to feel frustrated when I noticed a leather pouch near the microscope. It was long and flat and black and looked kind of like a pencil case.

I picked it up and unzipped it awkwardly. It was some kind of lab toolkit, and it contained a scalpel – I wouldn't have to dislocate my wrists after all!

I opened a desk drawer and stood the scalpel upright. Closing the drawer, I used my leg to keep the blade still. Then, carefully placing the rope against the blade, I moved my wrists up and down. It didn't slice through in one movement, but after a few nervous attempts, I did it. My hands were free!

Now all I had to do was find the right room. I slipped back out into the corridor. As I made my way further down it, a feeling of unease crept up between my shoulder blades, settling somewhere at the back of my brain, making my head tingle. I couldn't put my finger on why I felt this way. Maybe it was because I was getting closer to where James was imprisoned and I wasn't able to help him yet. But even as that thought crossed my mind, I knew that wasn't the only reason. There was something else – something I *wasn't* seeing.

As I moved forward, I had a vision of Iago doing the same thing, not that long ago. Then it came back to me – the torture labs had entry pads. Renny had used his lock-picking app to get into the first one, and Gek had opened the second one. I didn't need to check every room.

I raced towards the first door with a keypad next to the lock. That was the one with the lab-rats. That meant that the second door was the one with James in. I brushed my hand sadly along that one as I passed, whispering, 'I promise.' Then I came to the third one along. But that one had an entry pad too. Of course it needed an entry code – all the results of Gek and Faible's vile experiments were kept in here. They couldn't just allow anyone access.

I flipped my phone out, dialling Iago. He answered my call straight away. They were still in the taxi.

'I need Faible's entry code,' I said.

'What?' asked Iago. His voice crackled, the signal breaking up.

'I need the entry code,' I repeated.

'Tara – you're breaking up. Say it again.'

'I need Faible's entry code,' I said, louder than I wanted to.

If there *were* anyone within five hundred metres of this door, they would hear me. My voice echoed all along the corridor, swirling back towards me in long, low growls. It was too late to stop now.

'QUICK!' I shrieked, looking around.

'2802' shouted Iago in reply, mirroring my panic.

As I lifted my hand to the keypad, the sound I had been dreading came booming towards me. The unmistakeable sound of army boots heading my way. I tried the code. The red light didn't change. My fingers trembled so much that I had to stop and flex them before trying the entry code again.

'Tara – are you in yet?' Iago yelled.

This made me feel even more panicked. Suddenly the vision of the President in his hospital bed I'd had earlier flashed before my eyes.

'NOOOOO!' I screamed, banging the numbers into the keypad.

25

I was inside.

'I'll call you back when I find something,' I said to Iago.

'OK – I'll be waiting,' he answered.

I slid down the door after banging it closed behind me. I didn't dare turn on any overhead lights but there was a little light coming from the desk lamp. My throat was dry and my arms were shaking. I didn't know whether the guards had seen me entering the room, but I knew that it wouldn't take them long to find me. I had to find Faible's files and call Iago back as soon as I could. There was no point in them negotiating their way in to see the President if they didn't know which nanoviricides to give him.

Forcing myself to fight the worry building up inside me, I pushed myself back up on to my feet. Iago had said that the file was in a drawer. What kind of drawer? In films, the secret file is always in a locked desk drawer, so I decided to try the desk first. I scanned the room frantically, looking for something I could use to jimmy the lock. Rifling through the mound of paperwork on the desk, my hand came across something cold. It was a letter opener. I grabbed it, but my hands were trembling so hard, it rattled against the desk. I took a deep breath, trying to calm myself.

I tiptoed around the desk. Trying the top drawer first, I have to admit that I was a bit disappointed. It flew open easily as soon as I pulled the handle. The second drawer opened just as easily. Maybe I wasn't going to have the chance to test my spy skills. Nervously my hand hovered over the handle of the lowest drawer.

A loud clattering on the door made me jump. On instinct, my hand shot out and pulled at the drawer handle. The drawer flew open, almost coming off its rails. In my panic, I had used too much force. The noise it made boomed around the room.

I held my breath. Timed slowed, drifting like dandelion seeds blown by the wind.

I could hear faint noises outside the door – they were on to me. They were probably coordinating a plan of attack. I had to act. I was no match for those guys. If they got through the door before I found the file, the President would surely die. I couldn't let everyone down. I had to succeed.

Bending down, I began rifling through the bottom drawer. Adrenaline was flashing through my body, making my mind work quicker than my hands. Soon I realised that what I was looking for wasn't in the bottom drawer. Before I even stood up, my head was already scanning the room, looking for alternative search sites.

This was a pretty standard office; apart from the desk, there wasn't much in the way of furniture. With only the desk light on, I couldn't make out what else might be in the room. I ran back to the door, switching on the overhead lights.

'Idiot!' I hissed at myself. There — at the back of the office, were two filing cabinets. I raced around the desk to the nearest cabinet. Stretching up, I grabbed the handle of the middle drawer. To my complete horror, it didn't budge. I could hardly believe it — who locks filing cabinets? I suppose the answer to that is someone with secrets.

Letter opener already in hand, I attacked the lock at the top of the cabinet. Sheer, brute force managed to spring it open – there was no skill involved. Dragging the first drawer open, I stood on tiptoes to get a decent view of the contents.

The files were all labelled – 'Target A', 'Target B' and so on. How on earth was I supposed to know which file belonged to the President? I was furious. What was Faible up to? First, he forgot to take his files with him, then he forgot to mention that the lab door required an entry code. And now this!

Pulling my phone out of my pocket, I called Iago.

'That guy's up to something!' I shouted, as soon as he answered.

'What?' he asked.

'He's up to something... he... he's trying to trick you or something. He was hoping that I'd get caught before I got into his office. He doesn't want us to succeed.'

'Calm down Tara! What's got into you?'

'The files –they're anonymous.'

'What do you mean – anonymous?'

'I mean, I don't know which one belongs to the President. They all just say Target A or B or C. Do you understand? He doesn't want us to save the President.'

'Calm down, Tara. He's just an idiot. He probably

just forgot to tell me that his files aren't labelled.'

'No Iago – you can't trust him. You've got to believe me. He has a habit of forgetting important information, like his office needs an entry code, or that his files are anonymous.'

'You're right, Tara, but although I don't trust this man, right now, I have no choice. I have to hope that he does the right thing.'

'I understand,' I said.

'I know you're all alone and you're scared, but you could be the hero today. If you weren't inside the facility we wouldn't stand any chance of saving the President.'

'What's the name on the file?' I heard him ask.

There was a moment's silence and I worried that Faible wasn't going to tell us.

'Target T,' came Iago's voice.

'Of course it is!' I replied after pulling first the middle and then the bottom drawer open.

'What do you mean?' questioned Iago.

'It's in the other cabinet – just my luck. Listen – I'll have to get back to you.'

'OK – call me as soon as you can!'

I shoved the phone back inside my pocket and jammed the letter opener into the lock of the second filing cabinet. As I wiggled it with all my strength, there was an almighty bang on the lab door. Something was being rammed against it.

My heart leapt in my chest. I was seriously running out of time. My fingers fumbled and my wrists started to ache from the effort. As I struggled uselessly, my brain went into overdrive. I knew I had only seconds left. Swivelling the letter opener back and forth, I tried to guess which drawer the file would be in.

The next ram was so loud it made me squeal. Then I thought of Charlie, and James, and the President, and my mission. A real spook wouldn't give up, not now. I pulled my phone from my pocket and hit the camera icon. I laid it ready on top of the cabinet.

As the battering ram connected with the door for the third and final time, I jammed my knife into the lock, twisting with every fibre of my body. The drawer flew open at the same moment that the office door crashed inwards. As soon as my eyes located the file marked 'Target T', I flipped it open.

The guard stormed through the door. I had only time for one shot. As soon as the camera made the noise to indicate it had captured an image, I clicked 'Send photo'. Luckily, the last caller's contacts came up first. As I felt the guard's hand on my shoulder, I hit 'OK'. I prayed that it was the right information, because I was *not* going to be able to play any further part in saving the President.

26

Mr Steak-and-Eggs grabbed the phone from my hand, flinging it to the ground before stamping on it. *There goes my connection to the outside world!* I thought, and a shiver ran down my spine. Without a word, he hauled me to my feet, his big face puce with anger. I was turning out to be a bit of a thorn in his side, and I was starting to like it.

'It's not over yet!' I shouted as he dragged me towards the door.

He just laughed and I regretted my boldness. This intelligence officer thing was actually quite hard. Trying to keep the fear from showing on your face while you're shaking like a jelly is quite tricky. And nobody had pointed a gun at me or threatened to kill me yet. I needed to toughen up. I had to hold up under interrogation.

He pushed and pulled me back along the corridor. As we passed the reception area, I noticed that it was still empty. Was he the only guard left in the place? Maybe Iago had finally convinced the police to at least check the facility out. Why else would they have abandoned the place?

He dragged me into the lift and when we got to the first floor, he pushed me back out again, onto the mezzanine.

This time he didn't even bother trying to tie me down, he just shoved me through the door of Gek's big boardroom, slamming it shut behind me.

Stumbling forward, I tripped over the edge of the carpet, and landed face down. Luckily it was quite thick, but I still felt it graze my face as I slid forward.

'Tara – you OK?' came a frightened voice from across the room.

In my shock, it took me a while to work out who the voice belonged to.

'Aretha?' I gasped, lifting my head off the floor to look at my cousin, the pain suddenly forgotten.

She raced towards me, throwing her arms around my neck.

'Are you hurt?' she asked, looking at my grazed cheek.

'It's just a scratch,' I replied, sitting up. 'But... but what are you doing here? I mean – how did they find you? Oh no!' I broke off, suddenly terrified. 'Did they get Renny too?'

'No – they didn't,' Aretha replied. 'That's why I'm here.'

She paused and I stroked her arm, encouraging her to carry on.

'We were moving through the woods, trying to get away when we heard noises behind us. We knew it must have been Gek's men, and they were getting close. Renny was on the phone, trying to get that plane diverted. He was the important one and, well, I wasn't!'

'Hey – don't say that!' I soothed. 'You already saved our bacon earlier.'

'Anyway,' she carried on, her bottom lip trembling. 'I took the dog and made sure that we were seen. We led the guards away from Renny. Then he just left me...'

She began sobbing now and I realised that she was talking about the dog. He had betrayed her. What a mean, self-centred animal. Aretha had shown complete loyalty to him and as soon as it got a bit iffy, he bolted!

'C'mon now,' I said brightly, hoping to cheer her up. 'You've still got me. We may be in an awful mess, but we're still together. Has Renny managed to divert that plane yet?'

'He hadn't when I left him. He was getting really frustrated. His Geeksquad had managed to patch him through to the base at Incirlik. The problem was that no one wanted to listen to him.'

'What does he plan to do next?' I asked.

Aretha just shrugged her shoulders in response.

'Oh!' she remembered. 'He also mentioned that his Geeksquad found out there's a big family gathering at the Golden Strands casino this week.'

'What kind of family gathering?'

'I don't remember exactly who, but one of the big oil families. He said they control twenty per cent of the oil reserves in the Middle East.'

I gasped as the impact of Gek's latest plot became clear to me.

'If Evan Andrews gets anywhere near that Casino, Gek will be able to wipe out the entire family.'

Aretha gasped. I carried on.

'I don't know much about business but I'm pretty sure this would send the oil markets into a spin. I bet Gek plans to ride in there and threaten the owners of every other oil field, that if they don't sell him their rights for a song, they'll suffer the same fate.'

'They'd have to accept his offer,' she said.

The thought of that snake murdering and manipulating people for his own personal gain was making me feel sick.

'And what about all the other people – I mean the ordinary people that would become infected?' asked Aretha.

'You're right – the virus wouldn't only infect the oil family. It would spread to anyone with a similar genetic make-up!'

'That could be the whole population of Dubai!' she said, eyes widening.

'And, it wouldn't stop at the border – it could wipe out everyone on the Arabian Peninsula,' I said. 'They'd be what Gek would probably call *collateral damage*.'

I didn't want to frighten my cousin, but we'd been sitting there for a while and there was still no sign of the police. I didn't even know if Iago had managed to convince them to come here. I'd had no way of contacting anyone since my phone had been smashed and my rucksack taken from me. I looked around the room for a clock, but there was none. Even the big screens we'd watched the news on earlier had been switched off.

'What's that noise?' asked Aretha.

'What noise?' I asked, cocking my ear.

'Listen,' she said, turning her head slightly.

I followed her gaze. She was looking towards Gek's office space.

'It sounds a bit like a submarine diving alarm you'd

hear in a film, only much, much quieter. Can you hear it now?'

Now that she had told me what to listen for, I could hear it. It was very faint, so faint that it seemed to drift on the airwaves, sometimes disappearing altogether. But the more I listened, the clearer it became. It was definitely the sound of an alarm. And Aretha was right – it *did* sound a bit like the dive alarm on a submarine. I could almost see the film with some old wartime submariner shouting, 'Down periscope!'

The nagging feeling I'd had earlier returned. Something else was going on and I'd been too busy to notice it. Nervously, I dragged myself up off the carpet and crept cautiously towards the source of the sound. Grabbing my arm, Aretha kept close behind me. I could see that the room was empty, but something was different about it. Something *had* changed since I had last been in that room – not a huge change but it wasn't exactly the same.

Then I saw Gek's laptop open on his desk. That was it! It hadn't been there before. He'd taken it with him when he'd left the room. So he'd come back while I had been out looking for Faible's notes, but he wasn't here now. So why had he left his laptop behind?

'Is the sound coming from that?' asked Aretha, pointing to the laptop.

'I think so!' I replied.

I walked slowly towards it, Aretha now clinging to the back of my sweatshirt. We edged around the desk, still in human-train form. Although the laptop was open, the screen was angled down so that we couldn't see it. From this close, though, I could be sure that the noise we heard *was* coming from the computer.

As I reached down to push the screen up, Aretha tugged me back.

'No!' she whispered. 'Maybe we shouldn't. I mean – what if we find something...'

'Aretha,' I interrupted, 'ignoring things doesn't make them go away. You can't just stick your head in the sand – might get your tail blown off!'

I smiled and she relaxed a little, letting go of my top. Her fretting had made me nervous though, and my hands trembled as I reached for the laptop once again.

I had to force my hands forward. As I touched the screen, a spark of static electricity zapped from the computer to my finger, making me jump back and squeak at the same time. Aretha followed, jumping and squeaking just a split second after me. She put her hand over her mouth, embarrassed. I turned to smile at her. Then the look in her eyes changed. They widened until I could see white all around her deep-brown irises. She was staring over my shoulder at the laptop's screen. Whatever was on that screen had terrified my cousin.

I hardly dared turn around.

27

Aretha started backing away from the desk as I returned my attention to the laptop.

On the screen was a large digital clock, only it wasn't telling the time. Instead, the seconds were ticking backwards. It read 18.43. Behind the clock, in large red letters, four words flashed with every second that ticked by: Auto destruct sequence engaged.

'That *can* only mean one thing – can't it?' she said. 'I mean, *auto-destruct* usually means that something is set to destruct automatically. Doesn't it?'

I just nodded my head as I read the words flashing on the screen. I didn't know what was going to auto-destruct, but I presumed it wasn't just the laptop. This wasn't *Mission Impossible*.

My thoughts flashed back to Gek's vile face as he'd left me in this office earlier. He'd never intended to let me go. He didn't need this facility any more, but he couldn't just leave it. There'd be evidence of his heinous crimes. He wasn't worried about what the rest of the ARCTIC6 would say to the authorities. It wouldn't matter if they had no evidence. And he was going to make sure there was not a shred left to find. He was going to blow this place to high heaven – and anyone or anything still inside when it went up was going there too!

'We're going to die,' Aretha sobbed.

I didn't reply straight away. I just paced up and down in front of the desk, letting images shuffle through my brain... Iago... the President... Charlie... James. The first three I could do nothing to help, but I did have a chance to help James. I was still in the same building as him. I could still *try* to help him. That would take some effort though and *I* would need help!

'We are *not* going to die!' I said, thumping my fist on the desk, making the laptop jump slightly. 'Have you still got your phone?'

'Yes,' said Aretha, fishing her tiny NOVA smartphone out of her sock.

'Good girl!' I grinned at her.

My thought processes flowing now, I called Renny.

'Renny – I need your help!'

'Tara, is that you? Are you OK? What can I do?'

'We have a situation here and I think your Geeksquad might be able to do something.'

I was speaking calmly. I was in control now.

'My Geeksquad are pretty busy at the minute, Tar'. What do you need?'

'Do you know anyone who might be able to override an auto-destruct sequence?'

'*What?*' Renny's voice jumped an octave.

'We've got a problem here, Renny. Gek's computer is on the table in front of me and there's a warning flashing. It says "*Auto-destruct sequence engaged*".' I breathed in heavily. 'Do you think you can find someone to help us?'

'Say that again, Tara. No – wait, I heard you. I'm just

finding it hard to believe.'

'Can you help us, Renny?' I asked again, my lip trembling.

'Of course I can,' he answered. 'But who do you mean by "us"?'

'Me and Aretha,' I replied.

'Oh no!' my brother said. 'Listen – you guys just stay where you are. I'll find a way to help you. But I need you to answer some questions for me, OK?'

'OK!' I answered.

The concern in Renny's voice was making me feel a bit weak. I was worried that I might break down and cry. I breathed deeply again to steady myself.

'Is it a desktop computer or a laptop?' Renny asked.

'Laptop.'

'Is it connected to a modem or does it use Wi-Fi?'

I looked all around the laptop. I couldn't see any wires anywhere.

'Must be Wi-Fi,' I replied.

'Good!' he answered.

'Why?' I asked.

'Because it'll be easier to hack in through a Wi-Fi port. One of my Geeksquad runs what's called a "cloud-based hacking service".'

'What's a cloud-based hacking service, Renny?' I asked.

'It acquires Wi-Fi passwords. I should be able to get into the computer within twenty minutes.'

'What if we don't have twenty minutes?' I asked, looking down at the screen.

'We have to hope that we have that long, Tara. I can't guarantee it any quicker than that.'

'Well, Renny,' I replied, trying to sound calm. 'You'd better give your guy a call.'

'Why?

'Because we've only got seventeen!'

Renny was gone before I hit end call.

28

The key rattled in the outer door of the large boardroom. Was Mr Steak-and-Eggs back to tie us up in case we interfered with the auto-destruct sequence?

Aretha and I looked at each other. We were in enough trouble as it was. We couldn't afford to be tied up now. We needed to get out of here. We'd have to confront whoever was on the other side of that door, if we were to succeed. But we'd have to do it carefully.

Leaving Gek's office, we tiptoed quietly towards the outer door. Now we heard a light scratching noise – then silence. We stood frozen, waiting for the sound to resume. When it didn't, I stepped forward gingerly.

I looked all around the room for anything I could use as a weapon.

The door opened slightly, squeaking a little, then stopped. My heart began beating faster as I stood there by the door, defenceless. I looked around at Aretha – she also stood statue-like. She wasn't even breathing.

I realised that if we both just stood there, whoever was entering the room would have the element of surprise.

Throwing my hands out in front of me, I lunged for the door, hoping to shut it. Unfortunately, just before I reached it, whoever was on the other side had finally decided to enter. I tried to apply my brakes, but just like an out-of-control ice-skater, there was no way of stopping myself.

As my hands collided with the door, one of Newton's laws came into effect: I'll have to check with Renny which law it was. But I knew what it meant. My impact with the door would be as painful as our combined weights multiplied by our speed. Closing my eyes, I braced myself.

When the impact fizzled out shortly after my palm connected, I opened my eyes in surprise. There, standing at my feet, was none other than Aretha's disloyal dog.

'Oh dog,' called Aretha, running to him, throwing her arms out. 'You came back to save me. I knew you would.'

The devious animal nuzzled into her arms willingly, his eyes watching me all the while. He knew I wasn't fooled.

'I didn't know whether I could trust him or not,' came a voice through the open doorway.

'Cam!' we both screamed, running towards him as soon as he stepped into the room.

'Get off!' he groaned, as we both hugged him tightly.

Suddenly the world seemed a bit less frightening. Then I remembered our situation.

'Cam... how did you get here?' I asked.

'The dog showed me the way,' he replied, smiling.

I looked down at the animal by Aretha's feet. I'd been wrong about him. He hadn't abandoned Aretha in her hour of need, he'd gone to get help.

I bent down and patted him on the head. 'Good boy,' I said. I hope he knew I meant it.

He let out a tiny contented growl.

I turned my attention back to Cam. 'I didn't mean how did you find us. I meant what about Charlie? Why aren't you with her?'

'I wasn't doing any good just hanging around by her bedside. I was worried about you guys. Renny said that help was on the way, but it seemed to be taking a long time, so I called Charlie's uncle and told him what happened. I don't think he really believed me until he saw her. He's with her now and he's called the police, so they should be here soon.'

'How is she doing?' I whispered, almost afraid to ask.

'It's still too early to tell, but they said she was responding to the nanoviricides Faible gave her. We can only hope.'

'And pray,' said Aretha, closing her eyes.

'She's strong; she'll pull through,' he said, soothingly.

'Thanks for coming,' I said.

'Renny said you were in a bit of a pickle.'

'You could say that,' said Aretha, grabbing his sleeve. 'Oh Cam – it's really awful. Gek is going to destroy this place.'

'And everyone in it!' I added.

I didn't need to say any more. Cam understood what I meant.

'I know about the auto-destruct. Renny sent me a text just before I got here. Don't worry – he's the king of the geeks. He'll find a way to shut it down.'

'I just wish he'd hurry up,' said Aretha.

'He's got quite a lot on his plate at the moment,' replied Cam. 'C'mon, let's get out of here.'

I picked up the laptop and followed the others.

With Cam in the lead, we headed out of the door and back across the mezzanine towards the emergency stairwell.

As we ran, I asked him, 'What's going on with Renny?'

'He's having problems with the US military. He can't get them to turn the plane carrying Evan Andrews back to Incirlik. They just *will not* listen to him. They think he's some kind of crank caller.'

'Who will they believe then?' asked Aretha.

'No one *we* know,' said Cam.

'Not even Charlie's uncle?' I asked.

'No. He's just a helicopter rescue pilot – he doesn't have any authority. Renny says that since there's no evidence of a bomb on board, they won't listen. They're not worried about the virus in Somalia, because Andrews clearly arrived after the outbreaks had taken place. You remember that the virus killed almost instantly. And so far he's fine.'

'But there must be someone we can tell,' said Aretha, frustrated.

'But *who*?' asked Cam, pushing open the door to the emergency stairwell.

The dog bolted through first.

'I can't think of anyone,' Aretha whispered.

'Does Iago know?' I asked, suddenly.

'I think Iago's got enough to worry about,' he whispered, tiptoeing down the stairs.

'Have you heard from him lately?' Aretha asked.

'He's fine,' answered Cam. 'But he's not having much luck either. He was never going to convince the President's aides that a fifteen year old might be able to help. And Faible's credentials aren't exactly opening any doors. "Hello – I'm the man who created this deadly virus. Here – I have an antidote. All you have to do is trust me…" '

'Can't Iago put them in touch with the doctors who are treating Charlie?' I asked.

'He has. But Charlie's not really improving that much. They need something more.'

'They need some kind of evidence.' Aretha said. 'I mean – we need to show them the nanoviricides in action. Some kind of miracle.'

I carried on following Cam down the steps, turning over my cousin's statement in my mind.

'Aretha's right! We *need* to show them a miracle in action,' I said.

Cam stopped and stared into space for a moment.

'What is it, Cam?' I asked.

'You've just given me an idea,' he said.

I stared down at him. 'What do you mean?'

'We do a *Blue Peter*!'

'Huh?'

'We show them one we prepared earlier!'

'But we didn't prepare one earlier,' I replied.

'No, we didn't, but I'll bet Gek did,' Cam said.

'But we don't have time,' sighed Aretha.

I checked the laptop. 'Fourteen minutes left.'

'That's long enough!' said Cam. 'I'll call Iago.'

I hovered beside him, waiting impatiently while he called.

'Iago,' shouted Cam, 'Ask Faible if he ever filmed any experiments. Quick!'

29

'OK, thanks Iago,' said Cam, hanging up. 'They filmed the dog,' he said to us. 'The films are on Faible's computer in his office. How much time have we got left?'

Cam jumped down three steps and Aretha, the dog, and I followed without thinking.

'Thirteen minutes,' I answered, when we got to the bottom.

'Do we have time to get there and back?' he asked.

'If we're quick,' I answered.

'Look – you two don't have to come,' he said.

'I know the way to Faible's office,' I answered. 'But Aretha doesn't need to be here.'

'Hey! You've needed me more than once today,' said Aretha.

She was right.

'Let's go,' I said, exiting the stairwell and sprinting off down the corridor.

Cam caught up but Aretha stayed just behind, the dog with her – protecting her. The pounding of our feet was beginning to echo in waves down the long hall, each wave of sound colliding with the previous one, building a crescendo of noise that increased with every footstep.

I had to hope that the guards had left the building. With the auto-destruct countdown having a little over twelve minutes remaining, anyone with any sense would have got as far away as they possibly could.

Just as that thought ended, a dark shape appeared at the end of the corridor. I should have known better. It was Mr Steak-and-Eggs. He was probably on his last round, making sure that all the outer doors were securely locked, to prevent our escape.

None of us slowed one bit. At this stage, even fifteen stone of protein wasn't going to stop us. The life of the President rested on him getting the nanoviricides. If we couldn't prove to his aides that the nanoviricides worked, he would die!

The wall of flesh in front of us didn't move either as we drew closer. His eyes stayed focused straight ahead, only flitting slightly between Cam's face and mine. It seemed that he didn't consider Aretha a threat. That gave me an idea.

Slowing a little, I turned my head towards Aretha.

'Set the dog on him. He hasn't noticed him yet.'

We kept moving forward. When we got to about three metres away, I hissed, 'Now, Aretha!'

'Go boy,' she shouted.

With a speed normally only seen in wildcats, the dog flew past us, landing squarely on the security guard's chest. Mr Steak-and-Eggs was so surprised to be on the receiving end of another of this dog's defensive strikes that he lost his balance. He began staggering backwards, as the dog, clinging by his teeth to the front of the man's jacket, growled loudly.

After a while, the dog released his grip and dropped

to the floor. Pulling himself up to his full height, he growled, baring his teeth. The guard began backing away. I don't know whether he was frightened by the dog, or just didn't think we would make it out, but he turned on his heel and raced back down the corridor. *Well done, dog!*

Mr Steak-and-Eggs had slowed us down and we were in danger of running out of time. We needed to get a move on.

All three of us sped towards Faible's destroyed office door. As soon as we'd entered the room, Cam booted up Faible's computer. I drilled my nails on the desk while we waited. I couldn't help it; things were getting tight. Finally, the screen came to life.

'Do you know where to look?' I asked.

'I think I do,' said Cam.

I couldn't stay still; adrenaline was racing through my veins. I needed to do something. I grabbed Cam's phone off the desk and called Renny.

'Please tell me you're getting somewhere with this Wi-Fi hacking thing,' I shouted, more forcefully than I meant to.

'Honestly Tara – we're doing everything we can. I just got off the phone with Jinxie.'

'Who's Jinxie?' I cried.

'The cloud-based hacker I told you about earlier. Listen, we're all hoping that he can find a way of shortening the process just a little bit. If he can just give us one line of code to speed up the hack, we might be able to help you. But, if we can't – you guys need to get out of there! We'll keep working on the Wi-Fi, right up to the last second, but we can't promise anything.'

'Renny – I'm not leaving James and those animals in here to die.'

'Tara – you've got to think about yourself in this. I'm just telling you that I *can't* promise anything. We might not succeed.'

'The ARCTIC6 never give up!' I shouted.

30

'Come on!' I moaned at no one in particular. 'We're running out of time.'

'Calm down, Tara,' said Cam. 'Iago told me where to look. Don't worry – we'll find it.'

I was straining under the pressure. There were just so many things that needed to go right, and they had to be done in the right order. If we didn't find the files on Faible's computer then Iago couldn't show them to the President's security team. If the President's men wouldn't allow Faible to administer the nanoviricide, the President would die. If the President died...

'Oh that's it!' I said.

'What's it?' asked Cam, without turning his head. He was focused on searching through the files.

'If we can persuade the President's aides to use the nanoviricides, and if he recovers in time, maybe they'll believe us about Evan Andrews. Maybe then, the military will stop that flight that Evan Andrews is on. They'll *have* to believe us if the President gets better.'

We had to wake the President. If we didn't, Gek could threaten every oil producer in Arabia. And if they didn't agree to his terms, his virus would spread unchecked across the region.

And I knew one thing: this was only the beginning. Gek would target another population next. Genetic trait after genetic trait would be isolated. Bit by bit, he would *delete* the world's population. Wherever he saw something he wanted to possess, he'd simply murder the owners and take it! And, like the victims of his virus in Somalia, the rest of the world would believe they'd died of some new super-bug.

'Cam,' I asked, 'how are we doing?'

'I'm looking... I'm looking,' said Cam.

His hand was shaking so much that the mouse was jumping around the screen.

'I think I've got something. Tara, Aretha – have a look at this.'

We both leaned in closer. There was a film of a laboratory, with something like an operating table in the middle of it. Cam clicked on the fast-forward icon. Faible raced in and out of shot. The one constant was the dog lying still on the table, right in the centre of the screen.

Tubes dangled from its paws, their contents slowly dripping into its body. Through all the action, the dog never moved – never even blinked an eyelid. But it looked bad. It seemed to be on the verge of death. I could see its chest rise and fall very slowly as it struggled to breathe. Then I thought of James. This was what Gek had planned to do to him, if the experiment with his blood hadn't worked!

Cam stopped fast-forwarding. To my surprise, the dog started to look slightly better. Still there was no movement, no indication that it was conscious. I studied its chest. It was breathing faster, now. Then Faible shuffled into shot, head bowed.

'Turn it up!' I urged.

Cam searched for the volume control.

'*Tell them,*' came a voice from off-camera.

I didn't need to see who was speaking. I'd recognise Gek's cold-blooded lilt anywhere.

'*We administered the nanoviricide about—*' Faible checked his watch '*—about five minutes ago. As you can see, there are visible signs of improvement; heart rate is back to normal, blood pressure still slightly elevated, but that should come down soon. We even know that there is increased brain activity, although this one...*' Here he swung round, pointing at the dog, '*...this one's been through this before, he'll stay still, hoping to fool us.*'

Faible stopped speaking and stared at someone behind the camera.

'*Maybe we should have used the child?*' said Gek.

'*We didn't need to,*' answered Faible. '*Besides – you told me not to make human nanoviricides. You didn't want anyone to recover.*'

The camera closed in on the dog's face. This dog was more than just strangely familiar. I looked at the dog hovering nervously behind Aretha's legs. Was it him?

'That's it!' yelled Cam, startling me. 'That's the proof we need – let's go!

'Send it to Iago now and get Aretha out of here!' I shouted, racing for the door. 'There's something I have to do!

31

I was still counting on Renny coming through. I didn't have time to save the animals – James was my priority.

My legs pumped like a sprinter's. I puffed and panted, trying to get more oxygen into my bloodstream. I was getting tired – I knew that this was what my body needed – it's what athletes do to combat cramp. It wasn't working, but I carried on running as fast as I could.

Reaching the door to the room where James was being held, I stopped. I knew what I had to do. I was in control of this situation. All I had to do was go in there and get him out.

Punching in Faible's entry code, I opened the door. I stood in the entrance, anger pulsating from me like electricity. Nothing and nobody stood in my way, which was probably just as well. My senses in hyperdrive, I scanned the room. I knew that James was being kept in the nearest capsule on the left. But what about the other capsules?

With a thump of terror in my chest, I realised that none of us had thought about the other capsules in the room. What if there were other children being kept here? It had been so unspeakably horrible to see James imprisoned in that capsule that I'd never even considered the possibility that there might be others.

I could see a light above James's capsule, showing that it was switched on. Looking past it, I couldn't see any lights on the next one. So I turned my head to the right.

The first capsule didn't have any lights on. I had to step forward to see the second capsule properly. It was only one step, but it seemed to take forever. I held my breath.

Then I saw it.

There was a light above the second capsule.

Cam's phone vibrated in my pocket. My feet were frozen in place. Like an automaton, I pulled out the phone.

'What – is – it – Renny?'

'Tara – you sound weird! You all right?'

I didn't answer, so he continued. 'Listen, we're down to the wire, and Cam told me you took off. You *do* know that the chances of us succeeding, even with Jinxie's help, are less than hopeless?'

'Renny, please fix this!' I said. 'I need you now more than you know. Don't let me down.'

'Tara – please, I'm begging you. Get out now.'

'I'm with James,' I said.

'OK then – but hurry,' he replied. 'I'll do what I can.'

Surely, with all of his Geeksquad working together, Renny would come through?

I was suddenly terrified. I didn't want to look into that capsule. It was bad enough knowing that James was being kept inside one of these things.

Maybe there won't be anyone inside it, I said to myself. *The power could have just been left on by accident.*

I knew I was being optimistic. Why would the capsule be switched on?

One thing was certain – I had to look.

I stepped past the first capsule, looking into it on reflex. It was dark and it was empty. Although that was what I'd expected, I felt relieved.

The second capsule was only three feet away from the first, but it seemed to take ages to cross that distance. As I stepped in front of it, I looked through the glass door. I gasped not just in shock, but also in horror.

The child inside was smaller than James. It was a little girl, probably no more than nine years old. Her blonde head was slumped to one side. Her body hung limply from the restraints. Had she been drugged?

I remembered the men we'd seen getting out of the jeep. They'd carried something into the facility. Had it been this little girl? Had Gek needed her blood for some other hideous concoction of his?

Although she didn't look like she could move, she was conscious. Her eyes followed my face, as I moved closer to her capsule. When I pressed the release handle on the side, she groaned. My heart hurt. How could they do this – those evil men?

'Don't be frightened,' I smiled. 'I'm going to get you out of here.'

Reaching my arm out, I released the strap on her left arm. The child remained still – her body limp.

'What's your name?' I whispered.

'Sarah,' she answered.

'Sarah,' I said. 'I'm going to lift you out. OK?'

'OK,' she replied. Even her small smile took some

effort.

I put my arm around her waist to support her and freed her right arm. She shivered as I dragged her out of the capsule. She wasn't going to be able to walk. I'd have to carry her.

'Can you hang on to my neck?' I asked.

She clung on. I carried her, like this, over to James' capsule. Letting Sarah's legs down, I opened it.

'Can you walk, James?'

He tried to move his leg, but it was too stiff. He hadn't been able to move inside the capsule and his muscles had seized up. I tried to work out what I could do. He was bigger than Sarah. There was no way I could carry him. I could help him to walk, but not if I had to carry Sarah at the same time.

But time was ticking by. I had to act.

'I'll be back in a minute, James,' I said.

Then, picking Sarah up, I ran.

32

I didn't get very far.

This was useless. I just wasn't strong enough. I couldn't carry her any further. Defeated, I gently put her down and pulled out my phone.

'Aretha – put Cam on,' I shouted.

She passed him her phone.

'What is it, Tara?' he asked.

'Get back here and help me – NOW!'

'But you told us to leave?'

'There's another child,' I cried.

'What do you mean?'

'We didn't check the other capsules. There's another child. You need to help me.'

I could just about make out the click of his phone disconnecting, over the noise of my own footsteps as I hobbled towards the reception area, now dragging more than carrying Sarah.

Cam burst through the front doors and raced towards me.

I struggled forward as much as I could. We weren't moving very fast. But Cam was. He met us more than halfway down the corridor.

'Sarah, this is my brother, Cam. And he's going to

take you outside. OK?'

Sarah just nodded and Cam picked her up gently, whispering to me, 'Hurry, Tara.'

'Bad news from Renny?' I called as he started towards the entrance.

'No news!' he shouted over his shoulder.

No news is good news – I thought. *Or maybe not.*

As I raced back to the lab, I called Renny.

'Renny, please tell me you've found a way.'

'They've tried every dictionary they have,' he said. 'They can't crack the WPA.'

'What dictionaries are you talking about?' I asked.

'They need to find the Wi-Fi password. They do that by trying massive dictionaries of words and characters. If they can't crack the WPA, then I can't shut down the auto-destruct. Tara – where are you now?'

'Going back in. Why?'

'Well – I don't have access to the auto-destruct's countdown clock, but I did set a timer when you discovered Gek's horrible plan...'

'And?'

'And – well – you don't have long. I... I mean... you don't have long enough to get in and get out.'

My senses swirled and I felt a bit dizzy. I raced to the lab door again, punched in the entry code and headed for James's capsule.

He moaned softly as I took his arms, pulling him from the capsule. He was bigger than me, so I couldn't help him that much. I could only imagine the pain he was feeling as he put weight on his stiff legs.

Placing his arm across my shoulders, we staggered towards the door.

A loud siren like a ship's klaxon rang, making me stumble. As I tried to find my footing, James lost his balance. I couldn't stop the inevitable fall, so I threw myself underneath him to cushion the impact. We landed in a mangled heap on the floor.

As I struggled to get to my feet, my attention was drawn to a red light flashing just above the exit. Had it been flashing the last time I'd gone through it? I tried to convince myself that it might have been, but I'd been too busy to notice. Really though, I knew that it hadn't.

Before I could even move a muscle, the door underneath the flashing light began swinging shut. As the bolt engaged, the light stopped flashing. In its place was a fixed red glow – a clear signal that the door was locked. I didn't want to believe it. I raced to the door, pulling on the handle. Frantically, I yanked it up and down. It was no use. Even if the handle had opened, the massive steel bolt at the top of the door operated automatically. No amount of pushing or pulling would release it.

'Noooooo!' I cried, banging on the door.

Tears streamed down my face now, as I thought about what was going to happen. James and I were trapped inside this place. Now I knew that there was nothing I could do to help *us*. Fear struck my heart like a shard of ice. Defeated, I walked back to where James sat and sunk back down to the floor, taking his hand in mine.

'I'm sorry I couldn't save you, James,' I whispered.

'At least you got the girl out,' he said, hoarsely.

'Sarah,' I said. 'Her name is Sarah.'

James smiled and squeezed my hand. I'd done everything I could think of doing – there was nothing else I could do.

I still had Cam's phone with me though – I could still blog!

33

Arctic6blog9

I've done most of this blog on the fly. And I mean literally on the fly. For a while, when they took away my phone and iPad, I thought that I wasn't going to be able to keep you up to date. But, hope finds a way. And truth will out.

I know my situation is desperate, but I can still help. Even with nothing more than my phone, I can still communicate a message of hope.

There's a line in a poem by Keats that I've just remembered from English class. 'Beauty is truth, truth beauty, – that is all ye know on earth, and all ye need to know.'

The truth that we've uncovered here is far from beautiful, but I hope that out of all this horror something better will emerge. There are people who will use advances in science and technology to harm others. Still – that doesn't mean we should turn the clock back.

But only with leaders who really care about the future can we make a change. We need to think about more than just ourselves when we choose who leads our world. If they are not committed to making changes to clean up the environment and improve the lives of people everywhere on the planet, then don't vote for them. If you're not part of the solution, you're part of the problem.

But... enough about what I think. I'm still sitting here hoping for Jinxie to wave his magic wand.

I haven't got long now but Iago has recorded something that you need to hear, so I'm pasting the link in now. Please listen to what he says – it could mean the world one day...

'Hi – it's Iago again. This is becoming a bit of a habit, I know. But the truth is – I can't do it on my own. You can back out now if you want. Maybe nothing we do will make a difference, but I wanted to give you the choice.

Maybe you don't care about the President. Maybe you've been told that he doesn't represent you. Or you don't like the way he wears his hair, or the way he talks.

Sometimes I think that politics doesn't have anything to do with real life. The politicians seem to make such a mess of everything. They just go from one crisis to the next – if it's not a financial crisis, then it's a war, or an environmental disaster.

I know that between them they've managed to make a complete mess of our planet so far. But I DO believe that he is different. I know that we haven't seen much evidence of that yet, but I believe it WILL come. Might take some time though. You can't turn things around in a day. It took hundreds of years of greed and destruction to get us to this point. But we need to make changes today if we want to have any chance of reversing what's been done. It might take decades before we see any results.

And I'm afraid... really, really afraid, that this will

all stop if this man dies. I know that it's hard to believe that one man can change the world – but he can, if he embodies the hopes and dreams of everyone.

We need to wake him, not only because he represents something good in this world, but also because he can help us stop something bad – GEK!

That flight's getting closer to Dubai every second and if we can't wake the President they'll never turn it around.

We just can't allow Gek to annihilate any more people for his own benefit. Crazy, evil people shouldn't be allowed to control all the oil in the world.

I need to get back to Charlie now. She's still fighting. I know she's strong – but I need to see her face, hold her hand, talk to her! We've done all we can for the President. His aides finally agreed to try the nanoviricides. We don't know if they'll work. He'll still need to fight. He has a strong heart and his family are nearby. But they need your help...

You know that he lives with his Bluetooth in his ear – well, his wife has asked them to put it back in. She's switched his phone on and she wants you to call him. Yes, you – each and every single one of you. Renny's set up a message service if you can't get through. We won't stop taking your calls until he wakes up.

I know you're probably thinking – what on earth would I say to the President? But please don't think like that.

Just call him – say anything.

Just say hi, or tell him a joke. Try to reach him.

You never know – you could be the ONE... the one who wakes the President...

His number is 555-000000. Please call. Please call now!'

Hello – I'm sorry; the President can't take your call right now. But PLEASE leave a message for him...

'Hi Mr President. This is Gemma, from Oxford. I just wanted to say that I think you're right – we need to ban tuna fishing for a while. Otherwise, there'll be none left. Our future children and grandchildren shouldn't be denied something because of our greed.'

'Hello Mr President. This is Munesh from Calcutta. I think you are doing the right thing pushing forward investment in renewable energy. We all want to grow up in a cleaner world.'

'Hello. My name is Ola. I come from Zimbabwe. Thank you for trying to bring stability to our country. Please get better. This world needs you.'

'Hello Mr President. This is Andrea from Brazil. We love our rain forests and we are glad that you are working to convince people that we should protect them.'

'Hello. This is Sergei from Moscow...'

'Hello Mr President. This is Wei from Beijing...'

'Hi Mr President. This is Reinar from Bergen...'

...

...

'Hello – this is Renny. Who's speaking?'
'Um... it's Jake... Jake Niemand...'
'Hello Jake... you're through to the President...'

Epilogue

Arctic6blog10

Well, you did it again. I never doubted you for a second. There were a few anxious moments, when I wondered if anyone at all was listening. But Renny worked his mojo as usual and got Iago's message out there all over the web. His Geeksquad grows stronger by the day. He's actually having to turn down potential geeks now. Imagine – there might have to be some kind of interview process for future nerds wanting to offer their services.

Oh sorry! You probably want to know what happened...

As soon as Jake Niemand called the President, his eyelids fluttered. Don't know what you said, Jake, but the world owes you big time!

He didn't wake up immediately but the nanoviricides began to work. The doctors said it was remarkable – they'd never seen anyone fight so hard.

As soon as the President started to recover, his aides turned Evan Andrews' plane around. Andrews was eventually decontaminated, but he's devastated about infecting all those people, even though he was an innocent carrier.

Faible had nanoviricides for all the other G20 delegates, and luckily, no one else died.

That only left one dilemma for the ARCTIC6. Mine!

I sat there as the seconds ticked away, just holding James' hand in mine, hoping that someone would come and save us.

Anyway, however it happened – it worked. Jinxie came through. An obscure dictionary, consisting of no letters – only symbols – found the Wi-Fi password. Talk about eleventh hour – this was eleventh hour, fifty-ninth minute, fifty-ninth second stuff.

When the Wi-Fi cracker software found the password, Renny had less than one minute left on his countdown. And he didn't even know how accurate his countdown was.

He got inside Gek's system and, within seconds, he found the countdown file. Then, to his horror, he realised that the file was password protected.

He thought he'd failed. He said that for a second he thought he'd never see me again.

Renny doesn't fit in to normal life that well, but luckily for me, he excels at thinking outside the box. He was never going to find Gek's password in time, but he could use Gek's own medicine against him.

Renny launched a computer virus. He infected Gek's system with a worm. The worm opened its ravenous mouth and chomped through Gek's data in milliseconds. That countdown file went down in one bite!

It turns out that James and Sarah were both runaways. I said my goodbyes to them when the police finally caught up with what was going on. And I'm happy to say that they've now been reunited with their families and are doing fine.

Dr Faible went straight to prison and, despite helping Iago save the President, I think he'll be there for a long, long time.

And Charlie? I hear you ask. She was really bad. Iago rushed back to her bedside. Her parents had arrived by the time the rest of us got there.

I could see the fear in Iago's face. He didn't think she was going to make it. Iago, who I thought was the fighter among us, had given up.

We stayed by her bedside all night. By dawn, we'd all fallen asleep, Iago with his head on her bed.

But when I opened my eyes in the morning, I couldn't believe what I saw. Charlie was awake. Her smile was weak, but she was alive. I knew then that she'd pull through.

As for Gek, well I'd like to tell you that we tracked him down, but we didn't. He's probably back on the streets in some war-torn city, plotting and planning his next heinous crime. But don't worry. Renny's face-recognition software is better than the best, so if Gek even lifts his evil head above the parapet for a quick look, the ARCTIC6 will find him.

There is one final thing you might want to know about — the dog.

Well what could we do? He turned out to be a bit of a hero in the end. We were all sad to be seeing him go, but Aretha was totally devastated.

When we took him back to the old lady's cottage, she sobbed all the way up the garden path.

The old door creaked open, as before, and the ghost-like woman asked, 'What do you want?'

'I've brought your dog back,' answered Aretha.

The old woman shuffled forward and looked at the dog.

'I don't know this creature,' she answered, leaning over and staring into Aretha's eyes. 'But he knows you.'

Then she shut the door.

Aretha looked puzzled as she walked back towards us, the dog as ever, one step behind her.

'What shall we do with him now?' she asked.

'Since he seems to be yours,' said Iago, 'I think you should give him a name.'

'Oh thank you,' cried Aretha, hugging her brother.

'What are you going to call him?' asked Charlie.

'I think Joe's a good name for a dog,' I said.

'How about Gene?' sniggered Renny, enjoying his own joke.

'I thought Aretha was going to choose the name,' said Cam.

'So – what's it to be, sis'?' asked Iago.

Aretha grinned, and bent down to scratch the dog's head.

'Bandit!' she replied

The dog panted, waggling his tail happily. I think he was pleased with his new family and his new name.

And you never know – maybe he'll have a part to play in the next ARCTIC6 adventure.

COMING SOON . . .

www.arctic6.com

KILLER STAR

C T Furlong

an arctic6 adventure